Match Wits with The Hardy Boys®!

Collect the Original
Hardy Boys Mystery Stories®
by Franklin W. Dixon

Celebrate 60 Years with the World's Greatest Super Sleuths!

THE STING OF THE SCORPION

During Mr. Hardy's investigation of a ruthless gang of terrorists, Frank and Joe witness an explosion in the sky near an airborne dirigible owned by Quinn Air Fleet. They decide to look into the matter. The first clue takes them into a new animal park outside Bayport, where they are lured into a trap by an unknown enemy.

Pop Carter, the park's owner, has problems, too. He is being pressured into selling out by a competitor as well as a real-estate firm that wants the land for other purposes. At the same time, strange occurrences frighten both visitors and animals.

Frank and Joe are warned to stay out of the case, but follow up another clue. It leads them to an abandoned island, where they barely escape severe injury. When they return, they find a threatening message on their front door, written in an Oriental language. Do they have to contend with yet another adversary? They face danger from all sides, but their superior sleuthing skills and their courage win out in the end, when they unravel the threats of this many-faceted mystery.

Chet yelled in fright as he plunged to the ground.

The Hardy Boys Mystery Stories®

THE STING
OF THE
SCORPION

BY

FRANKLIN W. DIXON

GROSSET & DUNLAP
Publishers • New York
A member of The Putnam & Grosset Group

PRINTED ON RECYCLED PAPER

CONTENTS

THE STING
OF THE
SCORPION

CHAPTER I

An Elephant Vanishes

THE roar of an engine passing overhead vibrated through the Hardy house on Elm street one June morning.

"What in the world is that?" said Frank Hardy, who had just finished breakfast. "Sure doesn't sound like an airplane!"

"Let's find out!" exclaimed his younger brother. Blond and impetuous, Joe Hardy leaped up from the table.

Dark-haired Frank followed. They rushed out on the porch to peer up at the sky. A gleaming silver airship was sailing over Bayport.

"It's the *Safari Queen!*" shouted Joe.

"She was never that loud before." Frank frowned. "I wonder if they've got engine trouble?"

Seventeen-year-old Joe shaded his eyes against the sunshine and watched the huge airship anxiously, while his brother hurried inside for binoculars. The *Safari Queen,* biggest craft of its kind since the ill-fated *Hindenburg,* had aroused the keen interest and hopes of all lighter-than-air enthusiasts.

Frank returned and focused the glasses. "Oh, no!" he cried out. "Something fell out of the gondola!"

A vivid flash dazzled the boys' vision. A boom like thunder reached their ears, and billowing clouds of smoke blotted the airship from sight.

"Maybe the *Queen* exploded!" Joe gasped.

But the dirigible soon became visible again as the smoke cleared. Something else could be seen —and it caused the boys to stare in horror.

An elephant was plunging from the sky!

"I d-don't believe it!" stuttered Joe, who could discern the creature even without binoculars. The words were hardly out of his mouth when another explosion startled the brothers.

"The elephant blew up!" Frank exclaimed in a shocked voice. He lowered the glasses and the two boys exchanged stunned glances.

"I heard on the TV news that the *Queen* was bringing a load of wild African animals on this trip," Joe said, "for that new animal park, Wild World. But I never thought one would fall overboard!"

"If it really did," Frank added thoughtfully.

"What do you mean? We both saw it happen."

"Yes, but I was watching through binoculars and, you know, there was something funny about that elephant."

"Funny? What's funny about an animal blowing up?" Joe demanded indignantly.

"Nothing. But I'm not sure that it was a real animal."

"You think we were seeing things?"

"Of course not. But somehow that elephant looked—" Frank paused and scratched his head, "Well, I don't know, sort of stiff and unnatural."

"You mean, like a dummy?" Joe asked with an expression of quickening interest.

Frank nodded, frowning. "I guess so—a stuffed animal, or something like that."

"But why would anyone pull such a trick?"

"Search me. A publicity gimmick, maybe?"

Joe snapped his fingers. "Hey, that's an idea. Wild World just opened recently. Maybe someone thought this would attract customers to the park."

"Could be," Frank agreed. "But if you're right, I'd say whoever dreamed it up has weird taste in publicity stunts."

The dirigible seemed to be proceeding smoothly on course with no further sign of trouble. But the two explosions and the loud engine sound, compared to the *Queen's* normally silent flight, were alarming. The falling elephant added an even stranger touch.

"Let's go watch her land, and find out what happened!" Joe suggested.

"Good idea!"

The Hardy boys were fond of mysteries, and this one looked intriguing. They were heading for their car when the mailman came along. He had watched the startling sky scene, as had several other people in the area.

"What did you make of those blasts up there, fellows?" he asked, handing Joe a batch of letters.

"We can't figure them out," Joe replied. "But we intend to go and see."

"Leave it to you two." The postman chuckled.

Frank and Joe, both star athletes at Bayport High, were the sons of Fenton Hardy, a former New York City police detective who had retired from the force and was now a world-famous private investigator. His two boys already showed signs of following in their father's footsteps. Their most recent mystery, *The Firebird Rocket,* had taken the young sleuths to Australia on the trail of a missing space scientist.

Joe glanced through the letters the mailman had handed him and plucked out one addressed to The Hardy Boys. He went inside and tossed the others on the hall table, then hurried to join his brother, who was already easing their car down the drive. Soon they were bowling along toward the Quinn Air Fleet terminal, just north of town, where the airship would dock.

"Too bad this had to happen," Frank remarked as he steered the car through traffic. "Those explosions may start people thinking all over again that dirigibles are unsafe."

"True," Joe agreed. "It could set back the whole lighter-than-air movement."

The fiery crash of the *Hindenburg,* decades before, had ended dirigible development for many years. But the successful maiden voyage of the *Safari Queen,* which was the first of several such craft to be built for the Quinn Air Fleet, had raised hopes for a new generation of airships. Today's incident might dash those hopes.

As the boys approached the terminal, the number of cars heading toward the scene increased to a massive traffic jam, with drivers and passengers gawking at the fenced-in grounds of the Quinn Air Fleet base.

The dirigible was now nosed into her mooring mast, a stubby domed tower especially designed for quick, convenient debarking of the passengers.

"Looks okay," Joe reported, craning out the car window for a better view.

"Thank goodness," Frank said in relief. "I'll bet half these people thought they might see another *Hindenburg* disaster!"

The lines of traffic crawled, bumper to bumper, toward the terminal entrance. Just as the Hardys reached the intersection fronting the gates, the light changed to red. A policeman waved all cars away from the terminal, and the boys realized that their trip had been wasted.

The officer spotted them and came over to exchange a few words while they were stopped.

"I'm afraid you're out of luck, fellows. Can't let anyone else inside. Too big a tieup."

"Was the *Queen* damaged?" Frank asked.

"Nope. They haven't figured out yet what caused the explosions, but apparently they didn't do any harm."

"What about the elephant that fell overboard?" Joe put in.

"The word I get is, all animals are safe and accounted for," replied the officer, taking off his hat to mop his brow. "The whole thing's a total mystery—right up your alley."

"Boy, *what* a mystery!" Joe agreed.

"Say hello to your dad for me," the officer added.

"Will do," Frank promised as the light changed and the policeman walked off.

The boys were just getting past the worst of the traffic jam when a light flashed and the dashboard radio buzzer sounded. Joe switched on the speaker and lifted the mike. "Hardy here. Come in, please."

"G calling F and J." It was the voice of their spinster aunt, Fenton Hardy's sister Gertrude.

"What's up, Aunty?" Joe inquired.

"I've just had a code message from your father.

"You're out of luck, fellows. Can't let anyone else inside."

He wants you two to stand by for a phone call at one-thirty."

"We'll be there," Joe replied. "Any idea what it's about?"

"Something dangerous, I suspect," Miss Hardy stated darkly. "He said to beware of the scorpion's sting!"

"Okay, Aunt Gertrude, we'll be careful."

"See that you are! Over and out."

"What's that about a scorpion?" Frank asked, puzzled, as his brother hung up the mike.

"Search me. But that reminds me, we got another message this morning." From his hip pocket Joe pulled the letter that had come in the mail, and he tore open the envelope. Inside was a colored folder.

"Who's it from?" Frank inquired, his eyes still on the road ahead.

"There's no name or anything. Just a brochure from Wild World, the kind they hand out to visitors. Wait a second," Joe added as he opened the folder. "There *are* markings inside."

"Like what?"

"Well, there's a map of the park layout, and someone penciled in a diagram of the area right near the lion enclosure."

Frank pulled over to the curb to look. "What's this X-mark for, labeled 'hollow tree'?" He frowned.

"Maybe something's hidden inside the tree,"

Joe suggested, "and whoever sent this wants us to go there and find it."

"Funny way to tip us off."

"Sure is. It could be a practical joke."

Frank nodded. "But I think we should check it out. It may be connected with a case Dad's working on."

"Right."

Wild World was located on the coast of Barmet Bay, between the town of Bayport and the Quinn air terminal. Summer vacation had begun just a few days ago, and the park was crowded with people.

After driving through the entrance gateway, Frank turned left into one of the parking areas. He and Joe were getting out of their car when once again their radio buzzer sounded.

"Hardys here," Joe responded, almost expecting to hear another bulletin from their aunt.

Instead, a male voice came over the speaker. It sounded disguised. "If you want an important crime tip, meet me as soon as possible!"

"Who's this?"

"Never mind. Are you interested or not?"

Joe shot a glance at Frank, who nodded. "We're interested," the younger Hardy replied.

"Then go through the woods near the park opposite the entrance. Head for Spire Rock. It's a tall pointy rock formation, sticking up through the trees."

"We see it."

"I'll meet you there. Make it snappy. And don't tell anyone!" The transmission ended abruptly.

As Joe replaced the microphone, he looked questioningly at his brother. "Another practical joke?"

"We'll soon find out," Frank declared. "Let's go!"

Crossing the graveled parking lot, the boys plunged into the wooded area their unknown caller had indicated. They followed a narrow trail, winding among the trees. Suddenly they heard a rustling noise behind them. Before the Hardys could glance around, each felt something hard jammed against his back.

"Freeze—both of you!" a gruff voice barked in their ears. "One wrong move and you're dead!"

CHAPTER II

X Marks the Spot

FRANK and Joe glanced at each other from the corners of their eyes. Both were wondering the same thing. Had they walked into a trap, or was this the punch line of a joke someone was playing on them? In either case, was it safe to turn their heads and find out?

As if reading their minds, someone behind them—a different voice this time—snarled, "We don't want to hurt you, but the first one who tries looking around will get *this* bounced off his skull!"

A hand slid between them, displaying a nasty-looking leather-covered blackjack to emphasize the speaker's warning.

"Okay, we get the message," Frank said curtly. "What do you want?"

"Put your hands on your heads, where we can see 'em, and start walking toward those beech trees over to the left of the trail."

The boys obeyed, pressing forward through the dense vegetation without a word, though they were sizzling with anger. Each was ordered to lean against a tree, supporting himself with his upraised hands, as if for a police frisking.

"Now get this, and we'll only tell you once," the gruff voice warned. "You two keep your noses out of the *Safari Queen* trouble!"

"And don't take on any new cases," the second voice added threateningly. "Understand?"

"We heard you," Frank replied coldly, controlling his anger. "Is that all?"

"That's all for now, punk. Just remember what I said!"

The first voice chimed in again. "And don't turn around for the next five minutes. Just stay like you are—if you want to walk away from here alive!"

The Hardys listened as footsteps moved away from them through the underbrush. As soon as the sounds had faded, they glanced at each other, then lowered their hands and looked behind them.

"Those wise guys!" Joe fumed. "They may have been bluffing all along!"

"Maybe and maybe not." Frank shrugged. "They had the upper hand, and remember what Dad always says. No smart detective takes unnecessary chances."

"Think we should try to trail them?"

"And risk stumbling into another ambush? No thanks," Frank said. "With all this brush, we can see only a few yards in any direction. And think of all the people strolling around the park just beyond this screen of trees. How can we spot the guys who braced us when we don't even know what they look like?"

"You're right," Joe said bitterly. "But in that case, what chance have we to nail them?"

"Whoever they were, they must be mixed up in the *Safari Queen* mystery," his brother reasoned. "That gives us one lead to work on."

The Hardys decided to continue along the trail to Spire Rock, though it seemed certain the radio call had been a trick to set them up for what had just happened. The odd upthrusting rock formation was surrounded by a small clearing. Nearby was a public fountain at which a woman and two small children were drinking water.

No one else was in sight.

"Looks as if we wasted our time," grumbled Joe.

Just then three figures burst out of the bushes behind the boys.

"You wanted a crime tip—try this!" growled a voice, and the tip of a finger jabbed Joe hard in the ribs.

The Hardys whirled around, chuckling in spite of themselves. Both had recognized the voice of their chubby pal, Chet Morton. Two more of their high school buddies were with him, big rangy Biff Hooper and dark-haired, bookish Phil Cohen.

"Wow! Did you guys ever fall for that one!" Chet exulted. His plump cheeks jiggled as he bobbed up and down in sheer high spirits, poking Joe playfully.

"You're nuts!" Frank grinned. "You mean it was one of you who broadcast that phony radio message?"

"Who else?" Biff grinned back. "We saw you pull into the parking lot, and decided to feed you a little excitement."

"And you fell hook, line, and sinker!" Chet went on, rubbing it in. Then he paused to wipe the perspiration brought on by his cavorting from his moon-shaped face.

"After all," Phil added, "it's been at least a week since your last mystery, hasn't it?"

"That's what *you* think," Joe said wryly. "Matter of fact we've got a new one on our hands just since we left the parking lot."

Their friends were startled when they heard how the Hardys had been waylaid en route to Spire Rock.

"I don't get it," said Biff with a puzzled frown. "How could those hoods have known you'd be going through the woods just at that time?"

"They must have heard you broadcast the message," Joe deduced. "Where were you calling from?"

"The parking lot on the other side of the entrance you pulled into. Right after Phil spotted you, we used the CB radio in Tony Prito's pickup truck."

"Did you notice anyone eavesdropping?"

Biff looked at Phil and Chet. All three thought for a moment, then shook their heads.

"I guess not," Biff concluded. "But that doesn't prove much. There were people all around us, hopping in and out of cars. We were getting such a bang out of fooling you, we probably wouldn't have noticed, anyway."

"Where's Tony?" Frank inquired.

"He had to help his dad on some construction work." Biff explained that he and the others had come to Wild World to apply for jobs as park attendants in response to an ad in the Sunday paper. Although Tony had to leave as soon as they filled out their forms and were interviewed, Chet, Biff, and Phil had decided to stick around and enjoy the rides in the park's amusement area. "How about you guys?" he asked. "Did you come to apply, too?"

"Nope." Joe grinned, teasing. "We came to check out an X-mark on a map."

Their chums' curiosity was immediately aroused. When the Hardys showed them the mysterious folder that had arrived in the mail, their three friends insisted on coming with them to inspect the hollow tree.

Although Wild World was surrounded by a

high chain-link fence, the animal park proper was also partitioned off from the amusement area. To reach the spot indicated on the map, the Hardys' car would have to take its place in the line of vehicles cruising slowly along the road that wound through the animal range. A sign above the gateway warned spectators not to leave their cars.

"That X-mark better not be a gag," Chet grumbled as they paid their admission fare through the car window to an attendant with a coin changer on his belt. "This ride's costing us money."

"Don't worry. You'll get your money's worth just seeing the animals," Joe said.

"You bet!" Phil piped up enthusiastically. "I went through with my whole family a couple of weeks ago. It's almost like a trip through an African game preserve!"

His words were borne out as they passed in close view of grazing giraffes, ostriches, and gazelles. The sights were impressive. Many spectators pulled off the road to photograph the animals, and Joe wished he had brought his camera.

One ostrich gulped a peanut Biff tossed out the window. The creature seemed to take a fancy to him and raced alongside the car, keeping up easily with long loping strides of its knobby legs.

"Careful. I think it's fallen for you!" Frank joked. "Either that or it's hungry."

Biff hastily pulled back from the window. "Better get my head in before it gives me a peck on the cheek!"

"Serve you right for wasting good peanuts," said Chet, munching. He and Biff had each bought a bagful outside the gate, and the chubby youth was busily cracking the shells and popping goobers into his mouth.

"Boy, all you need's a good monkey suit, and you'd make a great addition to this park," Phil wisecracked.

"Listen, I haven't had a thing to eat since breakfast," Chet said defensively.

Joe glanced back from the front seat. "When was that, an hour ago?"

"Hey, we're coming to lion country!" Biff exclaimed, peering ahead over the Hardy boys' shoulders.

This area was enclosed by a fence of its own, and visitors were advised to keep their windows up. Frank, at the wheel, followed the cars ahead. Half a dozen or more of the big cats could be seen, including two males with flowing dark manes, several females, and at least one cub.

One male was fast asleep with his legs in the air, snoring audibly.

"Now that's what I call a real snooze!" Chet said enviously.

Frank grinned. "You should know."

He braked to a stop at the gate booth as they were leaving the lion enclosure.

"Can I help you?" said a black youth on duty in the booth. Pinned to the pocket of his green park attendant's uniform was a badge showing his name, Leroy Mitchell.

Frank took out the folder with the X-mark. "We're searching for a certain tree."

The youth glanced at the diagram, then looked up with an expression of puzzled interest. "Where'd you get this?"

"It came in the mail," Frank replied and showed him the envelope.

Leroy Mitchell's eyes widened. "Man alive! Don't tell me you're one of *those* dudes?"

"Which dudes?"

"The ones who solve all the mysteries—the sons of that famous detective."

"You guessed it. That's us," Frank said. "I'm Frank, and this is my brother Joe."

Leroy broke out in a friendly grin as he shook hands with the boys. "Wait till I tell everyone about meeting you two!"

"How about the tree," Frank asked, glancing around. "If I read this map right, it must be near here."

The black boy studied the diagram for a few moments. "Yeah, it's got to be that big old hollow oak." He pointed to a tree about a hundred yards off, on the right side of the road leading away from lion country.

"Okay if we get out and take a closer look at it?"

"Sure. I guess so. Nothing dangerous around there. But watch your step."

"Thanks, Leroy."

"Any time. Nice meeting you guys."

Frank drove near the hollow oak, then pulled to the side of the road. He and Joe got out.

"The rest of you had better wait in the car," Frank suggested.

Biff nodded. "Sure." He and his two friends in the back seat watched as the Hardy boys approached the oak.

"What do you think?" Joe asked his brother.

"Maybe there's something hidden in it." Frank stuck his arm in the hollow trunk.

"Anything there?" Joe asked eagerly.

"Yes, it feels like an envelope." Frank picked it up and withdrew his arm. As his hand came out, clutching the white object, Joe turned pale.

"Watch out!" the younger Hardy boy yelled. "Look what's on it!"

CHAPTER III

A Trumpeting Tusker

CLINGING to the envelope was a brown creature, several inches long. It had two crablike front claws, eight legs, and a tail ending in a stinger.

"A scorpion!" Frank gasped, his eyes widening in horrified disgust. The small animal's tail was curving forward over its back, ready to sting him in the hand. Frank dropped the envelope as if it were red hot!

The same question occurred to both boys.

"Is this what Dad was trying to warn us about?" Joe wondered out loud, still a trifle breathless.

Frank shrugged and ran his fingers through his hair. "Maybe, though I don't see how he could have known I'd stick my hand in this hollow tree."

"He might have known someone would use a scorpion sooner or later to harm us."

"Could be."

The loud sound of a put-putting motor caught the Hardys' attention. Turning, they saw a park guard speeding toward them on a trail bike. He had a visored uniform cap on his head and a holstered weapon on his hip.

Red-faced with annoyance, the burly officer braked his bike and swaggered up to growl at the Hardys. "What are you two kids doing out of your car?"

Joe started to explain, but Frank cut him short. "We got permission from one of the attendants."

"What attendant?" the guard demanded, as if he thought Frank were lying.

"Leroy Mitchell in the gate booth at lion country."

The guard turned to look in the direction Frank indicated. Leroy, evidently noticing that the Hardy Boys were in trouble, left his post and hurried toward them. Two or three passing cars slowed or halted so their occupants could see what was going on.

The guard started to bluster at the Hardys again as Leroy reached the scene.

"Take it easy," the black youth said to the officer. "I told them it would be all right to get out of their car just this once. They wanted to take a look at the tree."

"Don't you know it's against regulations for visitors to leave their cars?"

"Sure, but they only wanted to get out for a couple of minutes. And there's nothing dangerous around here."

The only animals in sight were a pair of mild-eyed gazelles, grazing and paying not the slightest attention to human goings-on.

"It's still against regulations," the officer said roughly.

"Okay. If I've done wrong, report me," Leroy said. "Don't hassle these guys."

The guard grunted and told the Hardys to go back to their car. "And from now on," he warned, "obey the park rules!"

Joe pointed to the brown creature crawling on the grass near the envelope. "If you're so anxious to protect visitors, better get rid of this scorpion before it stings someone."

The guard was taken aback and seemed reluctant to touch the odd creepy-crawler. Leroy grinned and brought an empty milk carton from his booth to scoop up the scorpion for safe disposal.

Frank retrieved the envelope, and after thanking the black youth, he and Joe rejoined their buddies in the car.

"What was that all about?" Biff asked.

Joe filled him and the others in as Frank peered inside the envelope. It contained a card bearing a seemingly senseless jumble of letters.

"Some kind of code," the elder Hardy boy declared and passed the card to his brother. "Guess we'll have to try cracking it later."

Joe studied the letters while Frank started the car and turned back onto the road.

"I wonder if the same party planted both this code message and the scorpion?" Joe mused.

"Good question," Phil agreed.

"There's another," Chet put in. "Would a scorpion sting kill you?"

"It would certainly hurt," Frank said, "and I think the venom of some species can be fatal. Matter of fact I intend to read up on scorpions in the encyclopedia when I get home."

"Likewise," said Joe.

"You really think someone planted that scorpion, and tried to set you guys up?" Phil inquired.

Frank shrugged. "I doubt that it got there on its own."

On either side of the road roamed zebras and several kinds of antelope, which the boys identified from the park folder as gnus, elands, and hartebeests.

Ahead, they were coming to a fenced-in elephant pen. Because the animals were big enough and strong enough to overturn a car, visitors were not allowed to enter their compound and could only drive past the fence, a few yards from the road.

Nevertheless, spectators were able to get an excellent view. Three of the huge beasts were drinking at a shallow creek that flowed through the enclosure. One was wading in the stream and scooping up water, then flipping its trunk backward for a do-it-yourself shower.

"I wouldn't mind cooling off like that," Chet observed enviously, fanning his chubby-cheeked face with the now-empty peanut bag.

"Why don't you get in there and join 'em?" Biff joked. "You'd look right at home—you're built along the same lines!"

"Don't knock it." Frank grinned. "That kind of beef makes a good football lineman."

Visitors' cars had slowed to a halt and everyone seemed to be enjoying the spectacle. In a foreign-made station wagon just ahead, a bearded man with a camera was waving and shouting to attract the elephant's attention, then hastily snapping pictures. Checking the rearview mirror, Frank noticed two men in sport shirts sitting in a blue car. They were wise-cracking loudly and chucking popcorn out the window at the elephants.

Suddenly one big tusker bellowed, taking everyone by surprise. The animal waved its upraised trunk to and fro as if sniffing the air, then charged toward the road, trumpeting loudly! When it reached the fence, the huge creature reared up on its hind legs, as if ready to batter down any obstruction!

"Oh, no!" Phil gasped. "Is that elephant powerful enough to break out?"

"Sure looks like it," Joe said, "if he gets worked up sufficiently."

The tusker's bellows of rage seemed loud enough to be heard all over the park. A guard speeded to the scene and summoned a trainer by walkie-talkie.

Presently a four-wheel-drive wagon appeared inside the compound. Evidently it had entered from the opposite side. It drove right across the creek and stopped about fifteen feet away from the angry elephant. The khaki-clad driver got out.

He began talking to the tusker in a coaxing, soothing voice and offered some tidbits on his outstretched hand. Gradually the enraged beast calmed down.

Chet glanced out the window. "Oh-oh," he muttered. "Here comes more trouble."

The guard who had scolded them earlier for inspecting the oak tree was striding toward their car. "Don't you guys ever learn!" he bawled at them angrily.

"What have we done now?" Joe demanded.

"I warned you once about obeying park rules! Now you're stirring up the elephants."

"Don't be ridiculous," Frank said, refusing to be bullied. "We were just sitting here, watching them."

"Yeah? And I suppose that big one got peeved because he didn't like somebody's face."

"Don't look at us," Frank said evenly.

"Don't get smart with me, kid!" the burly park guard stormed. "I'm going to teach you a lesson!"

"What's that supposed to mean?"

"It means you're all coming with me to the office. If I've got anything to say about it, this is a case for the police!"

He ordered the Hardys to follow him in their car while he escorted them across the grounds to a neat frame bungalow outside the fence. Here he made all five boys get out and took them into a room furnished with a desk and several file cabinets.

An elderly man with a tanned, weather-beaten complexion and white mustache listened calmly to the guard's ranting. Then he got up from his desk and shook hands with each of the boys.

"My name's Carter, fellows. Pop Carter, most people call me. I own Wild World. Glad you could come and see our animals today."

After the boys had introduced themselves, Mr. Carter added, "Is what the guard here says correct?"

"No, sir, it isn't," Frank replied. "It's true one of the elephants got worked up—"

The park owner nodded. "I know. I've already had a call from the trainer."

"But we didn't goad him in any way," Frank went on. "We were watching like the other spectators. If your guard was going to pick out anyone, why not the two men in the car behind us?

They were acting like wise guys and tossing popcorn toward the elephant pen."

"Not only them," Joe put in. "There was a black-bearded guy with a camera ahead of us, who kept waving and shouting at the elephants in a foreign language. He was trying to get them to face his way, I guess, so he could snap their pictures. Maybe that irritated them."

A strange expression appeared on the park owner's face. He glanced at the burly guard, who burst out, "They're trying to talk their way out! I think you should make an example of these smart alecks."

"All right, that'll do for now. I'll handle this," Pop Carter said calmly.

The guard left the office, red-faced and muttering. A moment later they heard his trail bike go put-putting off with a loud roar of exhaust.

Pop Carter grinned apologetically. "Sorry about that. He means well, but he has off days now and then. Got family problems, I guess."

The kindly old park owner tried to refund the boys' admission fares, but they refused his offer, having enjoyed their view of the animals despite the unpleasant episode.

"Mind answering a question?" Joe murmured hesitantly.

"I'll try, son," Pop replied. "Shoot."

"Why did you look so concerned when I mentioned the bearded foreigner?"

Mr. Carter eyed Joe in surprise and slowly filled his pipe. "You're quite a detective, my boy." Mention of the word detective seemed to strike him suddenly, causing him to do a double-take. "Wait a minute. You and your brother wouldn't be the sons of Fenton Hardy, by any chance?"

"We are, sir," Frank nodded. "Do you know Dad?"

"Met him once in Florida, when I was wintering there with the circus. Fine man. And I hear you two take after him."

Joe grinned. "Let's say we enjoy unraveling mysteries—or trying to."

Pop Carter seemed to make up his mind as he lit his pipe. "All right, here's one for you." He explained that the elephant, Sinbad, who had become enraged, was normally a peaceful, good-tempered animal and had only gone berserk once in the past. This had occurred when Pop was running a small circus and had hired a new trainer—a bearded Pakistani named Kassim Bey.

"Taking him on was one of the worst mistakes I ever made," Pop said, shaking his head reflectively. "Mind you, I've known other Pakistanis who were excellent with animals. But Kassim was just plain mean—he mistreated Sinbad and drove him crazy. I fired the no-good fellow as soon as I found out what had happened."

Kassim had reacted vindictively, cursing both Carter and Sinbad and vowing revenge.

"Said he was going to call down a Djinn or evil spirit to haunt us," Pop went on. "I paid no attention, of course, and Sinbad was a good elephant from then on. Behaved docilely at all times, up until a week or so ago, that is."

"Then what happened?" Frank asked.

"One night he started acting up again, trumpeting like all get-out. I live here, you see, and I could hear him, so I jumped out of bed and went to see what was wrong."

"What did you find?" Joe asked the elderly man.

"Nothing. Couldn't make out a thing, except —well, a dark shape soaring up and away through the trees."

"You don't mean one of those evil spirits that Kassim called down?" Frank inquired, half joking.

Pop Carter shrugged and looked at the Hardys with a sheepish grin. "I still don't know what to make of it. Maybe you two can solve the mystery."

CHAPTER IV

Wheel Trouble

THE boys were mystified by the park owner's story.

Pop Carter scratched his balding head and gave another helpless shrug. "Anyway, now Sinbad's thrown another tantrum. If it happens again, I may have to get rid of him," Pop added unhappily.

"Could those dirigible explosions this morning have upset him?" Joe suggested.

"I reckon it's possible. They were certainly loud enough around here. In fact, the airship was practically right over the park when it happened."

"Or maybe that bearded photographer reminded Sinbad of Kassim Bey," Frank put in.

"That's what I wondered at first," Pop admitted.

"Hey!" Joe snapped his fingers in sudden excitement. "Maybe that guy *was* Kassim Bey!"

Pop seemed momentarily startled by this idea. "What did this fellow you saw look like?" he inquired.

"Well, he had bushy black whiskers and a twirled-up handlebar mustache," Joe replied. "A big man, I think, although we never saw him out of his car."

The park owner shook his head thoughtfully. "Nope. Doesn't sound like Kassim. He had a slick black mustache that curved down on each side of his mouth and joined a neat little black chin beard. Above the mustache, he was clean-shaven."

Pop puffed on his pipe for a moment, then added with a sigh, as if annoyed at himself for taking the idea seriously, "Anyhow, it's impossible. I heard Kassim was killed in an accident after he left the circus."

From his worried expression, it seemed obvious to the Hardys and their friends that Mr. Carter had more on his mind than the elephant's misbehavior. The boys watched him as he moved away from his desk and stared out the window for a moment.

"Wild World seems to be quite a success," Frank remarked, breaking the silence. "Do you enjoy running an animal park more than a circus?"

"I love it," Pop said, turning back toward the visitors. "Put my life savings into this place. But now I'm wondering if I made a mistake."

"How come, sir?"

"Well, I opened the park in April, and I had Sinbad and his two mates brought here in May. Since then, it seems I've had nothing but trouble."

"What sort of trouble?" Chet inquired.

"First, someone tried to break into the park one night. The fence is wired, you see, so that set off an alarm. Upset all the animals and almost caused the giraffes and zebras to stampede. Terrible time we had getting 'em calmed down again. Then, later on, when the weather got warm, someone threw a stink bomb in the park on a real hot, crowded day. You can imagine what a commotion *that* caused!"

"I'll bet," Joe said sympathetically.

"Next, somebody started a rumor that the animals were rabid and might be dangerous to visitors."

"Hey, that's right. I remember hearing that," said Phil. "Did it lose you much business?"

"Sure did. Attendance fell way off for the next few days till I managed to get a full denial in the newspapers, and a clean bill of health from the State Wildlife Bureau." Pop spread his hands. "Why go on? It's been one thing after another. Sometimes I wonder if I wouldn't be smarter to sell out."

Frank's eyes narrowed with interest. "Has anyone made you an offer?"

"Sure. Matter of fact, two parties keep after me to sell."

"Mind telling us who they are?"

"One of them is Arthur Bixby. He owns several animal parks in other parts of the country, and now he wants to open one around here."

"Who's the other one?" Biff asked.

"Manager of a real-estate firm—fellow named Bohm. Clyde Bohm. Wants to develop this land around here as an industrial site, or some such."

Frank said, "Do you think one of them might be making trouble for you on purpose, trying to pressure you into selling out?"

Pop Carter tapped out the ashes from his pipe. "I won't say the idea hasn't crossed my mind. 'Course I can't prove anything. As far as facts are concerned, the whole thing's still a mystery."

"Joe and I will look into it," Frank promised.

"I'll sure appreciate it if you turn up anything."

Before the boys left his office, the elderly park owner insisted on giving them free passes to all the amusement rides.

Chet was ecstatic. "Wow! What a break! Let's try everything!"

His enthusiasm cooled, however, by the time they had sampled the first five. In fact, he appeared slightly green around the gills and decided to wait on a bench while his friends boarded the Ferris wheel.

Frank and Joe strapped themselves into one seat, with Biff and Phil facing them in the other. Presently the wheel began to turn.

"Wow! What a view!" Joe gasped. From the top of the wheel they could see not only the whole Wild World layout but most of Barmet Bay, with Rocky Isle clearly visible far out from shore.

"Know who invented the Ferris wheel?" Frank asked.

Biff grinned. "That's easy. A guy named Ferris."

"Wrong. It was William Somers, who built one in Atlantic City. Ferris copied it for an exposition in Chicago in 1893 and got all the credit."

To the boys' surprise, the wheel squeaked to a halt as their car reached the top for the third time.

"Something must be stuck," Phil said apprehensively.

Anxious minutes passed before the operator cupped his hands and shouted up that the drive mechanism had temporarily jammed but was now being fixed.

"Another headache for Pop Carter," Frank muttered.

The wheel soon began to revolve again, but the experience of being stranded helplessly in midair had been unnerving. Afterward, Biff and Phil went off in Chet's jalopy with a parting wave, while the Hardys drove home in their own car.

"Hmph! Late for lunch again," Aunt Gertrude observed as they entered the kitchen.

"We got hung up." Frank grinned.

The tall, angular woman was about to retort sharply when Joe added, "On a Ferris wheel."

"My stars! What happened?"

The boys described the amusement park mishap.

"Sounds suspicious, if you ask me," Miss Hardy commented. "If I'd been there, I'd have questioned the operator."

"We did," Frank told her. "He claimed it was just an accident, and that no one who doesn't work at the park had had any chance to tinker with the mechanism. We think he was telling the truth."

Their aunt eyed the boys shrewdly. "Are you two working on a new case?"

The boys winked at each other and nodded with a smile, well aware they had no chance of evading her cross-questioning. Besides, although Miss Hardy would never have admitted it, they knew what a thrill she got out of their detective work. They, in turn, enjoyed hearing their aunt's opinions, which more than once had given them a new angle on a mystery.

Over ham sandwiches and milk, followed by juicy wedges of apple pie, they told her about the anonymous letter and map that had led them to Wild World and the hollow tree incident. Miss Hardy was incensed when she heard how Frank and Joe had been waylaid in the woods when they first arrived at the animal park.

"I'd have taken a stick to those scoundrels!" she declared.

"I'll bet you would have," Frank said.

Just then the telephone rang, and he glanced at his watch. "One-thirty on the nose. That must be Dad!"

Both boys jumped up from the table. Frank hurried to the living-room phone, while Joe answered on the kitchen extension. Sure enough, it was their father, calling from St. Louis.

"What's up, Dad?" Frank inquired after switching on a scrambler to insure secrecy for their conversation. This synchronized with a portable device Fenton Hardy used whenever circumstances permitted.

The sleuth explained that he had been hired by the government to help round up a band of political terrorists known as the Scorpio gang.

"I've heard about them in the news!" said Joe. "They go in for bombings, don't they?"

"Among other things," Mr. Hardy replied drily. "But bombs are by no means their only weapons. They'll use any form of terror to hurt American companies or individuals they don't like." The gang's leader, he went on, was code-named the Scorpion.

"So that's what you meant by that warning in your radio message!" Frank exclaimed.

"Right, son. He knows I've been assigned to crack his gang, so he may well try to strike back at my family. I want you two to be on guard at all times."

"We will, Dad!" the boys promised.

Mr. Hardy related how he had zeroed in on the

gang's hideout in New York City more than a month ago, and had tipped off the FBI only to have the group escape moments before the police closed in. Since then he had been following up fresh leads in other parts of the country.

He was keenly interested when the boys told him of their morning adventures.

"I'd say there's no doubt the Scorpion himself was responsible for that park map you received in the mail," Fenton Hardy declared. "What's more, I believe the Quinn Air Fleet has been chosen as the gang's next target."

The owner of the airship service, Lloyd Quinn, he went on, had already received threatening messages. The messages called Quinn an imperialist tool and accused him of using the *Safari Queen* to help loot the resources of new African countries.

Mr. Hardy said he himself had been informed by the FBI about the dirigible explosions that morning, within minutes after they occurred.

"That's why I radioed you boys. I believe those explosions may be only the first move in the gang's war of nerves against Quinn. Now then, I'd like you to go out to the air terminal and talk to him. Scout for clues. You may be able to—"

The detective's voice broke off with a sudden gasp. "Hold it, sons! I think I'm being—"

Again his voice halted. The boys heard confused sounds, then a loud report.

Next moment the line went dead!

CHAPTER V

Queen of the Skies

"DAD! Dad!" Frank cried, jiggling the hook frantically. It was useless. The only response was a dial tone.

Hanging up, Frank went glumly back to the kitchen, where Joe greeted him with a worried look.

Noting their expressions, Aunt Gertrude demanded sharply, "What's going on? Is something wrong with your father?"

"He broke off the conversation suddenly, Aunty," Frank admitted, "but that doesn't mean he's in trouble."

Miss Hardy started to retort, then pursed her lips. "Hmph. Perhaps you're right. We'd better not alarm your mother."

Frank phoned the Quinn Air Fleet terminal and asked to speak to the head of the company, Mr. Lloyd Quinn. When he explained why he was calling, he was put through immediately.

Lloyd Quinn listened to Frank's opening remarks, then said, "The FBI told me about your father's investigation of the Scorpio gang, so I'll be happy to talk to you and your brother. If you can do anything to clear up this problem, believe me, I'll cooperate in every way possible."

"Could we see you this afternoon?" Frank asked.

"Any time. The sooner the better, as far as I'm concerned."

"Good. We'll be right over."

The terminal was a vast, sprawling complex of buildings, which included both an assembly plant and spacious maintenance hangars. It was also, in effect, an international airport. There was a reception building for passengers, with customs and immigration personnel to deal with incoming flights.

Dominating the whole scene was the mooring tower, with the huge, silvery, cigar-shaped *Safari Queen* floating majestically in full view.

"Boy, what a sight!" Joe exclaimed as they drove through the gate. "I wonder when the next airship in the fleet will be ready for its maiden voyage?"

"In a month or two, I think," said Frank.

Lloyd Quinn's office was in the reception building. After announcing themselves, the boys were whisked up by a private elevator and ushered in to see him. Quinn, a stocky, broad-shouldered man in shirt-sleeves, with a pug nose and a friendly grin, shook hands with the Hardys and invited them to sit down. His dress and manners were as plain as his office.

"What would you like to know, fellows?" he said, coming straight to the point.

"For one thing," Frank said, "have you any idea what caused those explosions this morning?"

"Grenades. Not much doubt about that. Someone aboard the *Safari Queen* dropped them just as she was arriving over Bayport."

"Any suspicions as to who that someone might be?"

Quinn shook his head. "Not really. But there are only two possibilities. Either a member of the crew was paid to do it, probably by this terrorist gang, or the grenades were tossed out by one of the passengers."

"How could a passenger throw something outside?"

"Through an emergency hatch. There are a number of them in the gondola. The *Queen's* not pressurized like a jetliner, you see. It cruises at much lower altitudes. In fact, it can drop down to rooftop height for sightseeing. That's one of the beauties of airship flight."

"What about the engine noise?" Joe put in. "It seemed a lot louder than usual."

Quinn smiled wryly. "It sure was. Normally she's as silent as a sky ghost. But some of the muffling came loose."

"Accidentally?"

"I'd be inclined to say yes if it hadn't happened just before those grenades went off. Under the circumstances, the answer may be sabotage."

Frank said, "Which would point to a crewman, right?"

"Right," Quinn agreed, with a troubled look.

"It fits in too neatly to be an accident," Joe pointed out. "First, the engine noise attracts people's attention and makes them look up at the sky, the way Frank and I did. Then they see and hear the grenade explosions."

"And the elephant falls out," Frank added. "Any idea how *that* stunt was pulled?"

"Not a hint," Quinn said, getting up from his desk to pace about angrily. "But the whole thing was fiendishly clever. It was purposely planned to give my air service a black eye and remind everyone of the *Hindenburg* disaster!"

Both Hardys had read about the fiery explosion of the famous German dirigible at Lakehurst, New Jersey, in 1937.

"That couldn't happen to the *Safari Queen,* could it?" Joe asked.

"Of course not. It wouldn't have happened to the *Hindenburg* if we'd let them have American helium gas, as they requested. We didn't, so they had to use highly flammable hydrogen. And even at that, what happened was no accident. More likely that, too, was caused by sabotage. But anyhow, the *Queen's* filled with helium, which can't burn. Most people don't realize it, but a helium-filled rigid airship is actually the safest method of air travel known to man."

"You really think dirigibles are coming back, sir?" Frank inquired.

"They're bound to," Quinn declared. "Not just because I'm a believer—the facts dictate it. Planes depend on airports, ships depend on seaports, and trucks depend on highways, but airships can haul anything anywhere, and do it cheaply, quickly, and safely."

"What about helicopters?" Joe questioned.

"Too costly and inefficient to operate, even if they were built big enough for real freighting. By comparison, the *Queen* can haul three hundred tons in a single trip, profitably." Quinn broke off with a boyish grin. "But don't get me started on all that. You're talking to a lighter-than-air enthusiast!"

He glanced proudly out the big picture window of his office at the *Safari Queen,* the first airship on the Quinn Air Fleet.

"Look at her. Isn't she beautiful? How would you fellows like to go aboard?"

"We'd love to!" the Hardys exclaimed.

In the elevator Frank asked, "By the way, were any of the African animals you were transporting here for Wild World harmed?"

"Not at all. They've all been inspected and safely trucked to the animal park."

The mooring tower was built with a projecting ramp, somewhat like the lip of a pouring spout. The nose of the dirigible rested atop this ramp, from which an extended walkway and conveyor led directly into the gondola, the cabin structure underneath the airship.

Quinn told the boys the *Safari Queen* was 600 feet long and could cruise at 150 miles per hour. It was powered by four turbines, which drove the main rotor and the blowers for the steering and hovering jets.

Frank and Joe were surprised by the spacious accommodations, which extended above the gondola well up into the main structure. The inside of the airship was not simply hollow and filled with gas, but divided into separate cells so that a sudden disastrous leak would be impossible.

As they went through the engine compartment, Joe noticed a young crewman who was eyeing them furtively. Without saying anything to the others, Joe snapped the fellow's picture with his miniature pocket camera, which he had brought along to photograph any clues that they might discover.

The aerial bridge, or flight deck, was a marvel of neatly arranged dials and control consoles.

"The ship can be flown from here to Africa entirely by autopilot," Quinn explained. "And the steering jets are computer-controlled to help counteract any crosswinds that might affect our course or stability."

The boys were thrilled at the view from the dirigible's wide cabin windows. "Sure gives you a lot better outlook than those peepholes on airliners!" Joe remarked.

Quinn smiled. "You bet they do! There's no finer sightseeing in the world than the view a traveler can enjoy on an airship voyage. And the Germans proved long ago that such trips can take place between continents on regular schedules, with no serious weather problems."

After showing the boys the *Safari Queen,* Quinn took them to his assembly plant, where a second dirigible, the *Arctic Queen,* was under construction.

"Where will this one fly?" Frank asked.

"To northwestern Canada, hauling supplies for a three-year pipeline project." Quinn's face darkened as he added, "That is, if what happened this morning doesn't cause the pipeline company to cancel our contract."

"You think they might, sir?"

"Who knows? Those explosions could arouse their fears about airship safety."

"Have you had any trouble before this?" Joe asked.

"Yes, two or three sabotage incidents."

Frank said, "Do you suspect anyone?"

Lloyd Quinn frowned and hesitated before replying. "Don't get me wrong. I'm not making accusations. But the only possible enemy I can

Joe snapped the fellow's picture with his miniature camera.

think of is a man named Basil Embrow. My former partner."

"The two of you broke up?"

"We had to," Quinn replied. "We were having
too many violent disagreements, so I went ahead
and formed this dirigible company on my own.
Embrow may bear me a grudge."

After asking for and obtaining computer printout data on the crew and passengers aboard the
Queen's morning flight, the Hardys returned
home.

Their mother informed them that they had received a phone call from Eustace Jarman, a well-
known New York industrialist and head of a large
corporation called Jarman Ventures.

"What did he want, Mom?"

"Actually, it was his secretary who called. She
didn't say what it was about, but left this number.
She wants you to call back."

Frank dialed the number, only to learn that
Jarman was out. His secretary asked if the boys
would be willing to come to New York City and
talk to him. An appointment was set up for eleven
thirty the next morning.

Afterward, Frank phoned Mr. Hardy's ace operative, Sam Radley, and asked him to trace
Quinn's ex-partner. Frank also read him the
names and other data on the twelve passengers
who had arrived in Bayport that morning from
Africa aboard the *Safari Queen*. All of them were
foreigners.

"Would you please find out if the FBI has anything on any of them?" Frank asked.

"Will do," Sam promised and rang off.

Meanwhile, Joe had developed and enlarged his photograph of the crewman. He had no special distinguishing features, except for a mole near his left eye. A check of their father's crime files revealed no data on him or any other member of the crew.

"Looks as if we're up against a blank wall." Joe sighed.

"For the moment, anyhow," Frank agreed.

The boys now set to work on the code message they had found in the envelope hidden in the hollow tree at Wild World. It read:

HXTREXST OCHOXTEH ROXCFUTX SVSKIETH

EEHYVSLA SXOXEDER HNRIXAXD

OOESAYWY ERXLMXIS

"There are quite a few X's," Joe mused. "Those could stand for spaces between words."

"Right," Frank said. "If you'll notice, there are exactly eight letters in each group—so those groups almost certainly don't stand for individual words as the message is now laid out. Hm, let's see."

A lengthy silence followed while the boys racked their brains for a possible key. Each tried various transposition and substitution ciphers without success.

"Wait a second!" Frank exclaimed suddenly.

"There are nine groups and eight letters in each group, which adds up to seventy-two."

"Hey, I get it!" Joe said. "You mean this may be one of those 'twisted path' ciphers, laid out in a square."

"Right."

The boys tried arranging the letters horizontally.

"That's it!" Frank exulted.

CHAPTER VI

Jungle Man

WITH the nine groups of letters laid out in rows, side by side, the Hardys had the following box:

HORSESHOE
XCOVEXNOR
THXSHOREX
ROCKYXISL
EXFIVEXAM
XTUESDAYX
SETTLEXWI
THXHARDYS

"In this case, it's not really a 'twisted path' cipher at all," Frank said. "Just a straight-line path."

"Check." Joe agreed. "Follow each line straight across from left to right, one after another, with the X's representing the spaces between words. Let's see what that gives us."

The deciphered message read:

HORSESHOE COVE NORTH SHORE ROCKY ISLE
FIVE AM TUESDAY SETTLE WITH HARDYS

The brothers looked at each other, and Joe whistled. "Settle with Hardys!" he read aloud. "That sounds like trouble!"

"It sure does," said Frank, frowning uneasily. "Seems as if enemies of ours are arranging a meeting to plot how to get even with us."

"Or get rid of us!"

"Right. The place will be Horseshoe Cove on the north shore of Rocky Isle, at five A.M. Tuesday—tomorrow morning."

"And the ones holding the meeting," Joe added, "could be this Scorpio gang that Dad's after."

Frank looked puzzled. "But that would go against Dad's theory. Remember, he suggested that it might be the Scorpion himself who sent us the park map in the mail—hoping one of us would get stung when we checked the hollow tree!"

"Yes. I'd forgotten that," Joe said, scratching his head. "But that doesn't add up either, Frank. Why would the Scorpion warn us about a plot by our enemies?"

"Maybe the warning's a phony. I mean this code message may be just a trick to lure us into a trap."

"In other words, if that scorpion in the tree didn't sting at least one of us, the gang would still get us when we go over to the island tomorrow morning to spy on their meeting."

"Right," Frank nodded. "But I think we should check out this information in the message, Joe, phony or otherwise. Only let's not wait till tomorrow morning. Let's go right after dark and keep watch tonight so they don't get a chance to set up a trap."

"Smart idea. And we'll take a couple of the fellows with us for extra muscle, just in case."

The boys hopped in their car and drove to the construction project, where they found Tony Prito jockeying a wheelbarrow full of cement. Tony, a dark-haired youth who had taken part in many of the Hardy Boys' mystery cases, readily agreed to accompany them to Rocky Isle.

"And how about taking your boat instead of the *Sleuth?*" Frank added, referring to the Hardys' own motorboat. "If this tip-off in the code message is a trick, the gang may be keeping watch on our boathouse to see if we take the bait."

"Smart thinking, Frank. The *Napoli's* all set for a run. I topped up her tank this morning."

From the construction site, the boys drove to the Morton farm on the outskirts of town. They found Chet's slim, pixy-faced sister, Iola, curled up on the front-porch swing, reading a book.

"Hi, Iola," said Joe, who rated her the cutest

girl at Bayport High School. "Where's Chet?"

"Out in that patch of woods behind the barn." She smiled. "He's busy on a new project."

"What now?" Frank asked. "Training squirrels to gather nuts?"

Though he avoided most forms of exertion, Chet developed a new hobby every few weeks. He would work at it furiously till the first flush of enthusiasm wore off, or an obstacle arose that threatened to require too much effort to overcome.

Iola giggled. "Go and ask him."

The Hardys tramped around the barn and into the wooded grove behind it. They found their roly-poly chum in T-shirt and gym pants, holding on to a rope tied to the branch of a tall tree and swinging.

At the sight of the brothers, Chet dropped to the ground. He was sweating profusely, but his moon face was wreathed in smiles.

"Hi, guys. Meet Jungle Man!" he thumped his barrel chest and gave vent to an errie bellow that shook the leaves on the trees.

"What in the world are you up to?" Joe asked.

"Wait till I tell you. Boy, have I got a great idea!"

"I'll bet."

"No, really! That setup at Wild World, it's really a form of show biz, right? I mean, the animal displays, and the amusement rides to help attract crowds. Pop Carter himself used to run a circus."

Frank shrugged. "I suppose you could call it a form of show biz. So what?"

"So I have an act that'll top everything!" their chubby chum announced.

"Chet Morton as Jungle Man?" Joe stared. "Are you kidding?"

"No. Let me give you a sneak preview!"

Chet spat on his palms, which were red and blistered. "I ought to rub some chalk on my hands first, but never mind."

He grabbed the dangling rope, took a few steps backward, then launched himself with a running jump. As he swung back and forth like a pendulum, he pumped with his chunky legs to increase the arc of his swing.

Finally he was far enough out to touch a tree behind him with his feet. Using its trunk to give himself a fresh push, Chet swung high in the air, aiming for the branch of another tree some distance away.

Unfortunately, the branch was too slender to support his weight, or perhaps it was already cracked from too much use. Whatever the reason, it suddenly gave way, just as he managed to land on it precariously.

With a loud report, the branch broke off. Chet yelled in fright as he plunged to the ground.

Luckily Frank and Joe had dashed to his aid as

soon as they saw the bough start to bend, so they were able to break his fall. But Chet was badly shaken by his mishap. "I think I need some nerve tonic!" he gulped.

"I think you're right, pal." Joe chuckled, and the boys went into the house.

Over ice-cold glasses of cola, the Hardys told their friend of their plan to spy out a possible enemy move on Rocky Isle. Chet tended to get the jitters whenever their mystery cases became too exciting, but could always be depended on in a tight spot.

"Okay," he agreed. "But let's play it careful, huh, and not go asking for trouble."

"We won't," Frank promised. "Anyway, it can't be any more dangerous than your jungle-man act."

Shortly after eight o'clock that night, equipped with sleeping bags and camping gear, the four boys shoved off from a dock in Bayport Harbor aboard Tony Prito's boat, the *Napoli*. A cool evening breeze had set in across the bay, carrying a bracing salt tang toward the shore.

"Should be great sleeping tonight," said Tony as he steered a course across the dark, moon-dappled water, kicking up plumes of spray.

"I just hope we *get* some sleep!" Chet remarked nervously.

Frank grinned. "We'll take turns standing watch. I wish it weren't so bright. But maybe it's just as well. At least we won't have to use our flashlights much to find our way around."

"Hey!" Joe exclaimed softly. "Speaking of flashlights, take a look over there!"

He pointed toward the brightly lighted amusement park area of Wild World, which could be seen overlooking the waterfront just north of town. A green light was flashing on and off from the revolving Ferris wheel.

"Somebody's signaling!" Chet Morton gasped.

CHAPTER VII

Cave Camp

TONY slowed the *Napoli* so they could watch the flashes.

"They're signals all right," Frank agreed, "but not in Morse code."

The same thought was going through everyone's head. Were the signals in any way connected with their secret scouting expedition to Rocky Isle?

"I don't like this," Chet gulped. "Maybe someone spotted us leaving the dock!"

"That's not likely," Joe argued. "Why would they watch Tony's boat? But I'll bet it has something to do with the gang."

Frank nodded thoughtfully. "I agree. If you'll notice, the flashes only occur around the top half of the wheel's turn, so the signals could probably be seen by someone on the island."

"Especially by someone on the north shore," Joe added, thinking of the code message.

"Want to turn back?" Tony asked in a disappointed voice.

"Not unless you fellows do," Frank said.

"Not me!" Tony declared with an air of suppressed excitement.

The Hardys glanced at Chet, who hesitated a moment, then shrugged cheerfully. "Oh, well, we've come this far. May as well see what's out there."

"Good," Frank said. "But from now on we'd better watch our step and be extra careful."

The green light flashes had ceased while they were talking. The boys continued their cruise to Rocky Isle, with only the sound of the boat engine and the slap of water against the hull to accompany their passage. As they neared the island, Tony shut off the motor and they made the final leg of the trip with muffled oars.

On Frank's suggestion, they beached the boat on the southwestern shore and covered it with brush and driftwood.

Rocky Isle was a popular picnic and swimming spot by day. The boys had briefly used a Chinese junk to operate a ferry service between there and Bayport. After dark the regular ferry service ceased, and the lighthouse was now automated, which left the island in desolate loneliness during the night hours. Even the park guard's cottage was dark.

"Let's leave our stuff here and scout the north shore before we settle down for the night," Frank said, after they had lugged their camping gear halfway across the island.

"Suits me," said Chet, who was beginning to puff a bit.

The boys hiked the rest of the way with their hands free except for flashlights, and cautiously probed the northern portion of the tiny island. The terrain was rocky and vegetation sparse, affording few places for cover.

The horseshoe-shaped cove was fringed by a sandy beach, which in turn was overlooked by flat-topped cliffs, barren except for weedy clumps of dune grass and here and there a gnarled, stunted tree. There was no sign of any other human in the area.

"We must have beaten the gang over here," Tony observed, "if they're coming at all."

"Sure looks that way," Joe agreed. "Let's bring our gear and lie down."

They unrolled their sleeping bags in the tall grass on the bluff overlooking Horseshoe Cove. A few boulders and a nearby tree gave them a certain amount of cover, and from this vantage point they could see anything happening on the beach below.

"We'll stand two-hour watches, okay?" Frank plucked several weed stalks, broke off the tops, and clutched four uneven pieces in his fist with the ends sticking out. "Draw straws for turns," he proposed. "Shortest stands the first watch, second shortest takes the second, and so on. Okay?"

Joe drew the first two-hour sentry assignment, and Tony the next, followed by Chet. Frank, who was left holding the longest straw, would stand the last watch, by the end of which time, the boys figured it would be daylight.

In the peaceful night air, with the sound of surf in their ears and the occasional distant mewing of seagulls, the three boys soon fell asleep. Joe was left to study the stars and keep his eyes and ears trained for any suspicious comings or goings. The lighthouse beam swept intermittently out to sea.

Some time later, Frank awoke in the darkness. He had heard a faint noise somewhere in the distance. Cautiously he squirmed upright out of his sleeping bag and looked around him.

Chet, who was guard at the time, was slumped against a rock. A low, sawing noise issued from his open mouth!

"Oh, no!" Frank muttered to himself. He wormed his way through the tall grass toward the edge of the cliff and scanned the shore, where a fresh shock awaited him.

On the beach, not far from a point just below his own position, he could make out the figures of three men!

Frank wriggled back toward his own group and shook their sleeping sentry.

"Chet, wake up!" he hissed, then immediately

clapped a hand over the boy's mouth before he could utter a startled outcry.

"Wh-wh-whassa matter?" Chet managed to say in a muffled voice between Frank's fingers.

"You fell asleep at the switch, that's what," Frank whispered in his ear, "and now three of the gang are down on the beach."

With the utmost caution, the pair woke up their two companions, and Frank, Joe, and Tony hastily pulled on their sneakers. Then, as silently as Indians, the boys wriggled toward the edge of the bluff. The three men appeared to be digging in the sand.

"What are they up to?" Joe whispered in his brother's ear.

"Search me."

Tony wormed his way closer to the brink of the cliff for a better look. In doing so, he dislodged a few fragments of gravel, which skittered down the steep slope! Instantly the three men on the beach jerked to attention. One swung a flashlight beam in the boys' direction.

"Someone's up there!" he shouted.

Frank realized that he and his pals might be in a tight spot if the men were armed. Thinking fast, he called out, "There they are, sergeant!"

Joe immediately clued in and exclaimed loudly, "I'll go get the rest of the men!"

Their ruse worked even better than they had dared hope. The crooks appeared to panic.

"It's the law!" one of them cried. "Let's get out of here!"

All three broke into a run down the beach.

"What do we d-do now?" Chet stammered, excited.

"Go after them!" Frank blurted. "Maybe we can scare them into surrender, or at least get a good look at them!"

The boys slid and scrambled down the steep slope and took off in hot pursuit, though the sand slowed their pace. The crooks were already out of sight in the darkness.

The shoreline curved sharply beyond the cove. As the boys rounded the arc of the horseshoe and continued along the jagged beach, they could see no sign of their quarry. Finally they halted to look around.

"Where did they go?" Tony asked, puzzled.

"They probably went up the hill to cut across the island," Frank conjectured. "The slope isn't that steep here. It wouldn't take them long to reach higher ground. I imagine they beached their boat a safe distance away, just as we did."

The four boys clambered back up the hillside for a better view. The moon drifted out from behind a veil of clouds, but despite the increased brightness, they could see no one.

Joe snapped his fingers. "Wait a second. I'll bet I know where they've gone!"

"Where?" Chet panted.

"That cave you discovered when we solved the Chinese Junk mystery!"

Frank was less hopeful, but agreed the cave might be worth looking at in the absence of any better leads. It was located on the north side of the island, not far from their present position. The boys walked toward it through the moonlit darkness.

To reach the entrance, they had to climb several yards below the brow of the cliff. Here Frank called a momentary halt before entering. They strained their ears for the slightest sound from within but could hear nothing.

"Okay, come on!" Frank led the way, keeping his fingers over the lens of the flashlight so as to provide just enough illumination to see where they were going, without glaringly advertising their approach.

Even in the dim glow of his flash beam, the interior of the cavern looked awesome. Because of water seepage, it was a "living cave" with glittering icicles that thickened into stalactites and stalagmites as the boys probed deeper into the bedrock of the island.

Finally the passageway widened into a huge chamber with a vast, greenish scum-laden pool that gave off faint ripples as water bubbled up from below. Frank shone his flashlight around more boldly now, convinced there was no one hiding in the cave.

"What's that?" Joe exclaimed, snapping on his own beam to brighten their view of a spot that Frank's light had just swept over.

There were unmistakable signs that someone had recently been camping there!

Excited, the boys skirted the small underground lake and hurried toward the far wall of the chamber. Besides a camp cot and a beat-up, greasy-looking pillow with uncovered striped ticking, there were several cartons of canned food along with eating utensils, bottled beverages, a kerosene lantern, and a supply of candles and matches. Accumulated trash from a number of meals lay nearby.

"Whoever the guy is, or was, he must have been here for more than a few days," said Tony. "He left plenty of empties."

Frank picked up a book from the cot. Its title was *Elephant Lore*. "Joe, look at this!" he exclaimed. "The guy's been reading about elephants!"

The Hardys traded startled glances, each remembering what Pop Carter had told them about his recent difficulties with Sinbad.

"And that's not all," Frank added suddenly as he leafed through the book. "What do you make of these?" He pulled out two snapshots that had been stuck between the pages.

"Jumpin' catfish!" Joe gasped. "They're pictures of *us!*"

Tony and Chet crowded closer and stared at the photographs.

"Not very good shots," Tony observed.

"Don't worry. We never posed for them," Frank said wryly. "These are telephoto shots, snapped on the street when we didn't even know our picture was being tak—"

He broke off as Chet suddenly clutched his arm and hissed, "Shhh! I think I heard something!"

The Hardys instantly doused their lights. A moment later, a shot blasted the darkness!

CHAPTER VIII

A Dangerous Dummy

KAPOW! The bullet ricocheted off a stalagmite close by. The cavern rang with echoes and all four boys sank to the ground.

"Spread out!" Frank whispered urgently.

More shots followed, spraying the area where they had just been standing.

Joe snatched a hunk of rock from the floor and pegged it hard in the direction of the last gun-flash.

He was rewarded by a yelp of pain and, almost at the same instant, the splashing sound of something falling into the water.

Silence ensued, the boys scarcely daring to breathe. Tense moments lengthened. Then suddenly the stillness was broken by footsteps running away through the cavern.

Was their enemy's retreat just a trick? The four teenagers wondered.

At long last, Frank groped for a rock and ventured to flash his light, ready to douse it again instantly and hurl his missile, should his beam reveal a glimpse of their unknown assailant.

There was no one in sight!

He played the light around thoroughly to make sure the gunman was not hiding behind a thick stalagmite or rock formation.

"All clear, I guess," he murmured.

The four boys rose warily to their feet, and Frank's companions switched on their own flashlights.

"Whew! Wh-what an experience!" Chet quavered. "I might have known something like this would happen, once you Hardys started chasing clues!"

"Thank goodness you heard the guy in time. You probably saved us," Frank congratulated their plump chum. He added to his brother, "Nice going on your part, too, Joe. I take it you heaved a rock at him. At least that's how it sounded."

"Right. I guess I hit him."

"Yes. And then he must've dropped his gun in the pool."

"So he decided to get out fast before we got him." Tony chuckled in relief.

The boys retraced their steps to the cavern entrance, moving carefully, ready to react at any moment if their enemy was lying in wait.

As they emerged into the night air, the faint drone of a boat engine reached their ears. They listened as the sound slowly faded in the distance.

Joe glanced at his brother. "Think that was the crooks leaving?"

Frank nodded. "Probably."

The Hardys went back into the cavern long enough to retrieve the elephant book and snapshots, as well as the eating utensils, the lantern, and one of the empty soft-drink bottles.

"These should be enough to give us some clear fingerprints of the man who was hiding in the cave," Frank declared.

They ripped open the pillow ticking and used it as a makeshift bag to carry the evidence. After the Hardys rejoined their pals, the boys trekked back to Horseshoe Cove. Here they shone their flashlights around the site where the three men had been digging.

A seated figure startled them momentarily, but Frank waved reassuringly. "Relax. It's only a dummy."

The dummy's back was propped against the cliffside, in a slight shallow recess formed by two projecting rocky outcrops.

"Why did they plant *that* here?" Joe wondered. He started to move forward to examine the seated figure, when Frank stopped him, flinging his arm across Joe's chest.

"Hold it! There's your answer!" Frank pointed

to a round disklike object that Joe had almost stepped on.

It was made of green plastic and was about the size of a small Frisbee. Apparently the men had been burying it in the sand when Tony's move had alerted them to the presence of watchers on the cliff.

"What's that?" Chet blurted.

"A land mine, unless I miss my guess." With cautious fingers, Frank unearthed the device. Under Mr. Hardy's expert training, he had learned how to recognize and disarm such contrivances. He took no chances, treating this one with the utmost respect.

Luckily he saw a pressure switch lying in the sand close by and realized the crooks had not had time enough to rig a detonator.

"A booby-trap setup?" Joe questioned, shaken.

"Right. That's why the dummy was put here. To arouse our curiosity. After walking up to examine it, one of us would have stepped on the mine, and—*boom!*"

"Whew!" Joe wiped his forehead. "And I almost did!"

"It wasn't fixed to go off yet," Frank reassured him.

"Thank goodness!"

"Also, from the looks of this," Frank went on, "I'd say it doesn't contain enough explosive to do more than stun us, or at worst, injure us slightly."

"Then what was their angle?" Tony asked.

The older Hardy boy theorized that the code message had been carefully planted as bait for the booby trap. "They figured we'd know enough about secret codes to decipher the note. Then when we got here, the mine would either scare us off the case or disable us enough to be captured without a fight."

"In which event," Joe added, "they would have held us as hostages to force *Dad* off the case."

"Correct," Frank agreed.

There was silence as the four youths digested the grim significance of their find.

Finally Tony stretched and sighed. "What do we do now?" he asked. "Hit the sack again or go back to Bayport?"

"May as well go back," Frank advised. "We've accomplished what we came to do."

"That suits me fine," said Chet. "I've had enough of this creepy place!"

Before leaving the island, the boys stuck a note under the park guard's cottage door, informing him that a man who might be involved in criminal activities had been hiding out in the cave. Then they lugged their camping gear to the *Napoli* and climbed in. As they headed back across the bay, the first pearly light of dawn streaked the horizon.

Joe was silent and thoughtful as they entered the harbor. "Do you suppose those three hoods came to Bayport after they left the island?" he asked his brother.

Frank shrugged. "Hard to say. They seemed to be heading down the coast, but the way sound spreads out over water, it's hard to judge direction. Why?"

"Remember why we went in Tony's boat instead of our own?"

"Sure. We figured the gang might be watching the *Sleuth* to see if we took the bait."

"Right," said Joe. "So if those hoods didn't come back here and report what happened, our boathouse may still be staked out!"

Frank's eyes narrowed. "That's an idea! If we move fast, maybe we can nab the guy who's keeping watch!"

"And make him talk," Joe added grimly.

As soon as they had entered the marina and tied up at the dock, the Hardys left Tony and Chet to unload the *Napoli* while they themselves hurried off along the waterfront to check out their hunch.

They were still fifty yards or more from their destination when Frank suddenly flung out his hand in warning. "Joe, look!"

A man was tampering with the lock of their boathouse door!

CHAPTER IX

Sky Show

In unspoken accord, Frank and Joe quickened their pace, preparing to grab the trespasser before he could get away. But he evidently heard their footsteps pounding across the wharf.

The man turned with a startled expression. Then he let go of the lock and darted away. The boys got only a quick glimpse, but noticed that he was dark-complected and had a black mustache.

The two young sleuths gave chase.

Their quarry was heading for a dockside warehouse. Barrels, crates, and empty oil drums were crowded against the front wall. Just before rounding the corner of the building, the stranger knocked over two of the drums with a sweep of his arm and sent them rolling toward the boys.

"Look out, Joe!" Frank yelled.

The younger Hardy tried to sidestep hastily,

lost his balance, and fell, sprawling headlong on the wharf! Frank himself had to dodge the rolling drums, and by the time the boys resumed the chase, the fugitive was out of sight.

"Come on. We've got to catch him!" Frank urged.

As they ran around the side of the warehouse, they suddenly saw the intruder.

"There he goes!" Joe yelled.

The mustached man sprinted across a parking lot and then an open field, heading for a street that ran parallel to the waterfront.

Just then a bus came into view, filled with workers on their way to early-morning jobs in Bayport. The man turned toward a bus stop straight ahead.

"Oh, no!" Joe groaned as the boys redoubled their speed.

The bus rolled to a halt and the man leaped aboard.

"Stop, thief!" Frank shouted at the top of his lungs.

But apparently his words failed to carry. The bus doors swung shut, and despite the Hardys' frantic waving, the vehicle sped off toward town.

The Hardys skidded to an angry halt. "Of all the luck!" Joe fumed, socking his fist into his open palm. "Think there's any sense getting out our car and trying to follow the bus?"

Frank shook his head in disgust. "It's already out of sight, and our car is way over at the marina.

By the time we catch up, if we ever do, the bus will be unloading downtown. And for all we know, that guy might jump off at the first stop."

Glumly the young sleuths rejoined their two chums, loaded their sleeping bags and other items into their car, and drove home.

Aunt Gertrude, as usual, was up bright and early, and so was their slender, attractive mother. Both women listened attentively while the boys recounted their night's adventure.

"What about that explosive whatchamacallit the crooks were hiding in the sand?" Aunt Gertrude inquired.

"We dropped it overboard in the deep water on the way back to Bayport," Joe informed her.

Miss Hardy nodded approvingly, then pursed her lips. "Those criminals may strike again."

"You're right," Frank agreed. "That's why we've got to nail them. If we can identify any fingerprints on this stuff we brought back from the cave, at least the police will know whom to look for."

"Smart work," Mrs. Hardy said. "I'll make breakfast now. Then you two had better get some sleep."

"I could sure go for bacon and eggs," said Joe. "But I don't feel like turning in just now. Guess I'm too keyed up."

"Same here," Frank said. "We have to go to New York this morning to see Eustace Jarman, the business tycoon. We can doze on the bus."

Both brothers wolfed down a hearty breakfast, then set to work in their basement lab, dusting the objects from the cave with powder. Much to their surprise and disappointment, there were no fingerprints on any of them.

"That guy must've wiped everything he touched," Joe grumbled.

Frank nodded. "He was playing it safe and taking no chances in case anyone discovered his hideout."

"Which means that he must be a pro."

"I'd say there's no doubt about it."

The boys showered, changed their clothes, and started out for New York City. It was only a few minutes after eleven o'clock when their bus rolled into the Port Authority Terminal, which gave them ample time to keep their eleven thirty appointment at Jarman's midtown office. The weather was bright and sunny.

"Let's walk," Frank suggested.

"Good idea."

The sidewalks were filled with the usual bustling crowds. Noting the bumper-to-bumper crosstown traffic, Joe chuckled. "We're probably making better time on foot than we would by taxi."

A ripple of gasps and excited remarks ran through the throng of pedestrians, and the boys suddenly noticed people stopping to stare skyward.

"Hey, look!" Joe exclaimed.

A sleek, silvery airship was gliding majestically over Manhattan!

"The *Safari Queen!*" said Frank.

Awed, excited comments could be heard all around them.

"I'll bet Quinn sent her here to prove that nothing serious happened yesterday," the older Hardy boy guessed, "and to show everyone his dirigible's as good as ever."

"If that's his idea, it's working," Joe said. "Listen to the way everyone's admiring her."

The words were hardly out of his mouth when two baby blimps suddenly soared up into view.

"Hey! Where'd they come from?" Joe asked.

"A skyscraper up ahead," said Frank. "They must have been berthed on the roof."

"The two mini-airships headed straight for the *Safari Queen.* They looped and swooped and maneuvered about the larger craft like baby whales frolicking around their mother. The sidewalk observers chortled with delight at the spectacle.

"What a show!" Joe chuckled.

"I doubt if the *Queen's* pilot appreciates their company," said Frank. "But the crowd really goes for it. I wonder who thought *this* one up?"

"I don't know, but I intend to get some pictures while the show's on!" Joe took his miniature camera from his pocket and began snapping photographs rapidly.

The boys finally walked on as the dirigible

sailed southeast toward Brooklyn and Long Island. At the Jarman building, they took the elevator to the industrialist's penthouse office. A smiling, beautifully dressed secretary ushered them in.

Jarman was a tall, intense-looking man with long dark hair and a hawklike profile—the perfect picture of a hard-driving business executive. He got up from behind his huge modern desk to shake hands with Frank and Joe.

"Glad you fellows could come. I'm sorry I was out when you returned my call yesterday."

"What was it you wanted to see us about, Mr. Jarman?" Frank asked when they were all seated.

"My security department's been in touch with the FBI about the activities of those confounded terrorists, the Scorpio gang," Jarman explained. "I gather you Hardys are working on the case."

"Dad is, sir. We're helping unofficially," Frank replied.

"That's good enough for me. From what I've heard about you two, your 'unofficial help' is often mighty effective."

"Did you want us to investigate something, Mr. Jarman?" Joe inquired.

"Yes," the businessman said emphatically. "If you're not already working full time to run down those terrorists, I'll pay you to do so."

"Thank you, sir, but there's no need for that," said Frank. "In fact, I doubt if it would be right

"I wonder who thought this one up?" Frank asked.

for us to accept such an assignment from you, since Dad's already in charge of the case. But, as I say, we're working with him, and Joe and I intend to do all we can to help catch the Scorpio gang. May I ask what your interest is in the case?"

"Jarman Ventures is a vast corporation. We do business in many fields, and we've already had several brushes with terrorists. But that's not all." Jarman clipped off the end of a long cigar, lit it, and eyed the boys with a thoughtful frown as he blew out a cloud of smoke. "I'm sure anything I tell you will be kept confidential."

Frank and Joe nodded. "Of course."

"The fact is, Jarman Ventures is moving into the lighter-than-air field."

"You're building a dirigible yourself?" Joe asked with keen interest.

The businessman nodded. "My aircraft division has already laid the keel of one even larger than Quinn's. It'll be called the *Globe Girdler* to indicate its worldwide flight range. So naturally I'm pretty angry over what happened yesterday."

"You mean," Frank said, "the bad publicity?"

"Exactly. Anything harmful to *his* dirigible is bound to affect my project, too. That's why I want to do anything I can to help nab these filthy terrorists. And that's why I contacted you two."

"Believe me, sir," Frank declared, "we're as anxious to round up the Scorpio gang as you are. And we'll be happy to follow up any leads you can provide."

"Good. Then I'll instruct my security department to pass along any clues they uncover."

"What got you interested in the lighter-than-air field, Mr. Jarman?" Joe inquired.

"The tremendous future I see for it. Matter of fact, we've been building blimps, which are non-rigid airships, for several years."

The Hardys exchanged surprised grins.

"Those little ones we saw this morning wouldn't be yours by any chance, would they?" Joe inquired.

"You bet they would!" Eustace Jarman replied with a pleased smile. "I keep them berthed right here on the roof of this skyscraper."

He got up from his desk again and strolled across the room to gaze out the huge floor-to-ceiling window of his penthouse office.

"Here they come now!" he said.

Frank and Joe both joined the industrialist. Looking east, they could see the two little craft over Manhattan.

"I got the idea of sending them up on the spur of the moment, when the *Safari Queen* appeared over New York," Jarman related proudly. "Then I had my public-relations department phone all the news agencies and TV networks."

"It made a terrific spectacle," Frank said, genuinely impressed.

"I knew it would," the tycoon boasted. "Unless I miss my guess, that scene will show up in news photos clear across the country. I expect it to generate as much publicity as those dirigible explosions yesterday morning."

Jarman glanced at his watch, and the boys got the impression they were politely being dismissed. "I wish I could have lunch with you fellows, but I'm booked with some European manufacturers. You'll have to excuse me. This is a high-pressure schedule I work under."

He strode to his desk and picked up a pen. "Let me write you a check, though, to cover your time in coming here today."

When the Hardys declined, Jarman promised to take them for a ride personally in one of his baby blimps on Thursday, and asked them to meet him at Bayport Airport at noon.

"We'll really enjoy that, Mr. Jarman," Frank said, shaking hands.

After leaving the tycoon's office, the Hardys went down to the lobby.

"There are phone booths up ahead." Joe pointed. "Maybe we ought to call home and see if anything's happened."

"Good idea. I hope they've heard from Dad!" Frank found enough coins in his pocket to cover the call and dialed the Hardys' area code and home number. After depositing the amount of money requested by the operator, he was put through.

Aunt Gertrude's voice came on the line. "Hardy residence," she said crisply.

"This is Frank, Aunt Gertrude. We're still in New York."

"Well, make it brief. These long-distance calls cost money!"

"You're telling me." Frank grinned as he looked at his depleted stock of coins. "We just wanted to find out if anything has come up while we were gone."

"Yes. You had a call from Sam Radley. It sounded important. He wants you boys to phone him right away!"

CHAPTER X

Mole Mystery

"Okay, Aunt Gertrude, I'll ring Sam as soon as I hang up." Frank hesitated uneasily before adding, "No word yet from Dad, I suppose?"

"No, indeed—we've heard nothing so far." Miss Hardy's voice reflected her own anxiety. Then she reverted to her usual tart tone, like a top sergeant bracing up recruits. "But I don't want you boys to worry about him. Do you understand? Just mind your own p's and q's, especially in a city as big as New York. The streets are dangerous these days, from all I hear. As for Fenton, he can take care of himself!"

"Thanks, Aunty, we'll bear that in mind," Frank said, comforted in spite of himself by her brisk, no-nonsense manner. "Tell Mother we'll be home soon. 'Bye now."

He replaced the receiver in its cradle and shook his head in response to Joe's questioning glance.

"She says they haven't heard from Dad. But we're to call Sam Radley, which means I'd better get some more coins."

After breaking a bill at a drugstore news counter, just off the lobby, Frank returned to the phone with his brother and rang his father's long-time operative.

"Hi, Sam. This is Frank," he said when the detective answered. "Aunt Gertrude gave us your message. Got something for us?"

"Sure have," Radley replied. "I've traced Quinn's ex-partner, Basil Embrow."

"Nice going. What's the scoop?"

"He's now running a business called Embrow Exports in Manhattan. I figured you two might want to check him out while you were there."

"Right. We'll do that. What's the address?"

The operative read it over the phone and Frank copied it down. "Thanks a lot, Sam," he said and hung up.

"Lower Manhattan," Joe noted, glancing at what Frank had written. "We can take the subway."

Leaving the building, the boys were thrilled to see the two baby blimps directly overhead. The minicraft were just about to settle into their berths on the penthouse deck, high atop the skyscraper.

"Boy, I can hardly wait to ride in one of those things," Joe said eagerly.

"Right. They're tubby little cigars, but they do look like fun."

The Hardys took a subway train downtown. Embrow Exports occupied a tenth-floor suite of offices in a dingy area, but the firm looked busy and prosperous.

"I'm not sure Mr. Embrow can see you," a receptionist told the boys. "Have you an appointment?"

"No, but give him this, please," Frank said. He wrote something on a slip of paper and handed it to the young woman, who excused herself and took the message to her employer.

Joe shot his brother a quizzical glance. "What did you write?" he asked in a low voice.

"Just 'Quinn Air Fleet.' Let's see if it works."

Apparently it did. The receptionist soon returned and said that Mr. Embrow would see them.

The businessman wore a puzzled frown as the boys were ushered into his office. "What's this supposed to mean?" he asked, flicking his fingernail at the paper.

"Nothing in particular. It's the only thing I could think of that might get us an interview," Frank replied.

Embrow, a balding, raw-boned man, responded with a smile to Frank's boyish grin. "Fair enough. At least you're honest. Sit down and tell me what I can do for you. Am I mistaken in thinking you two are the sons of that famous detective?"

"No, sir, you guessed right," Joe replied. "Fenton Hardy's our father. In fact that's why we're here. We're helping him on one of his cases."

"Indeed? What sort of case?"

"It has to do with those dirigible explosions yesterday morning," Frank replied.

Embrow sighed, nodded, and settled back in his chair. "I see. I thought there might be some connection." He rolled a pencil back and forth between his palms for a moment and frowned. "Well, what would you like to know? Do I take it I'm under suspicion?"

"Why should you think that?" Frank inquired.

"Look! Let's not play games. I'm sure you've found out by this time that I used to be Lloyd Quinn's partner and that we broke up after a quarrel. Why else would you be here?"

"Naturally we have to check out every angle," Frank said.

"Sure, I understand that. But if you think I had anything to do with those explosions, you're barking up the wrong tree."

"Any comment you'd care to make about the case, Mr. Embrow?"

"Just one. No. Make that two. First, I hope you Hardys catch whoever's responsible. And second, I wish Lloyd Quinn nothing but good luck." Embrow grinned at the boys' wary expressions and added, "Does that surprise you?"

Joe grinned back. "Well, it's not exactly the sort of attitude we were led to expect."

"I can imagine. Lloyd and I are both hot-tempered guys. We went at it hammer and tongs before we busted up. But that's water over the dam. I've got too much going for me right here to waste any time harboring grudges."

"How did you two meet?" Joe asked curiously.

"We served in the Navy together," Embrow replied. "In blimps, on Atlantic-patrol duty. That's what got us interested in dirigibles. We both made up our minds that someday we'd go into the field commercially."

"Do you regret leaving?"

"Frankly, sometimes I do. It's an exciting field with a great future. On the other hand, my export business has been highly successful, and I must say, I don't envy Lloyd any of his present headaches."

Joe nodded at a framed desk photograph that Embrow had been toying with as he spoke. It showed a youth in an academic cap and gown. "Is that your son?"

"Yup, it's his high-school graduation picture." Basil Embrow smiled proudly. "Quite a lad if I do say so, though I don't see much of him these days." He moved the photograph aside with a brisk back-to-business gesture and said, "Well, is there anything else I can tell you fellows?"

"No, sir. You've answered all our questions," Frank replied, rising. "We appreciate your frankness."

"And thanks for your time," Joe added.

The boys shook hands with Embrow and left. Outside the building, they headed back to the subway entrance, a couple of blocks away.

"What do you think?" Joe asked his brother.

Frank shrugged. "Hard to say, but he seems a decent enough guy."

"I agree. He's not my idea of a sneaky saboteur."

"By the way, why did you ask him about that high-school picture?"

Joe's eyes twinkled. "Don't tell me you didn't spot it?"

"Spot what?"

"That mole next to the boy's left eye."

Frank stopped short with a gasp. "Now I get it! Just like that Quinn air crewman you photographed who was giving us the once-over!"

"Check. I snapped a shot of Embrow's desk photo, too, with my pocket camera."

"Good work!"

As soon as the boys arrived in Bayport, Joe developed his roll of film. Then he enlarged the picture of the youth in the desk photo and compared it with his shot of the air crewman.

"Hmm. The mole's in the same place," Frank mused, "and their faces are similar, but I'd hate to bet they're the same person."

"Ditto," Joe agreed. "Besides, there's at least five or six years' difference in ages, and neither one of these blowups is ideal for identification purposes. Also, the name stenciled on the crewman's coveralls isn't Embrow. It's H. Maris."

"Which could be phony," Frank pointed out. "He'd hardly apply for a job under his own name if there were enmity between his father and Quinn, especially if he were planning to sabotage the *Safari Queen*."

"True, but it's not that easy to get the kind of fake ID he'd need, like a social-security number and maybe a birth certificate and so on. Unless—wait a minute!" Joe snapped his fingers. "Do you suppose there might have been someone else filling in yesterday, doing some temporary maintenance work, and wearing Maris's coveralls?"

"Let's find out." Frank picked up the phone, dialed the Quinn Air Fleet number, and was soon talking to Lloyd Quinn himself. But the air-fleet owner said no temporary help was ever employed, partly for security reasons and partly because of the high degree of specialized training needed for dirigible work.

"I had a call this morning from that pipeline company," Quinn added glumly. "The one my next airship was supposed to haul supplies for. Needless to say, they heard about the midair explosions yesterday, and the way they're talking now, they may cancel our contract, just as I feared."

"At least it hasn't happened yet," Frank said,

refusing to be discouraged. "We'll do our best to crack the case before it does happen."

He hung up without mentioning his family's fears for his father's safety.

Meanwhile, Joe was studying the computer printout data on the crew.

"Look. It says here Maris attended Ardvor College," he remarked after listening to Frank's report. "Why don't we drop over there tomorrow and see what we can find out about the guy?"

"Good idea."

Just then the phone rang. Frank picked up the handset and answered. His face burst into a happy smile as he heard the voice at the other end of the line.

"Dad! We've been worried about you. Are you all right?"

"Yes, son. I'm calling from Cleveland. Sorry I had to end our last conversation so abruptly."

"What happened, Dad?" Joe put in. He had realized that Frank was speaking to their father and now he eagerly crowded close to the receiver.

"I discovered I was being watched," Mr. Hardy replied.

"By whom?"

"A known terrorist. At least that's who he looked like. I was calling on an airport phone. When he saw I'd spotted him, he snatched a traveler's bag and hurled it at me, and then got away in the confusion."

"You think the guy's a member of the Scorpio gang?"

"It's possible. The odd thing is, he was reported to have fled this country over a year ago. He's a Hindu named Jemal Raman, and at that time I was investigating him for acts of terrorism against his own government's embassies over here."

Fenton Hardy explained that he had gathered enough evidence against Raman so that the U. S. Immigration Service was preparing to deport him. But before a hearing could be held, the Hindu escaped aboard a freighter, evidently fearing arrest.

After listening to the boys' report of their own activities, the detective advised them to keep an eye out for Raman. "He could be vengeful and dangerous. Better check him out in my files."

"Will do, Dad," Frank promised. After hanging up, he got Jemal Raman's dossier from the crime file in his father's office so he and Joe could study its contents. These included three long-range telephotos, snapped without the subject's awareness. They showed Raman to be dark-skinned, with a drooping mustache.

"Do you suppose this could be the snoop we spotted at our boathouse this morning?" Frank asked, with a glance at his brother.

"Sure looks like him." Joe was startled as he examined the photos closely. "Jumping catfish!

Notice how his mustache curves down on each side of his mouth?"

"What about it?"

"With a black chin-beard, this guy might even fit Pop Carter's description of that elephant trainer, Kassim Bey!"

Before Frank could reply, a scream rang through the house!

CHAPTER XI

The Knobby-Nosed Peddler

"THAT's mother!" Frank cried.

Joe dropped the photos and both boys dashed into the kitchen. They found their mother backing away from a huge scorpion!

The horrid-looking creature, now poised on the kitchen counter, was brown and hairy and about six inches long. Mrs. Hardy, pale, stared at it with a shocked expression, holding one hand over her mouth. In her other hand she held a wide-mouthed plastic container.

"Out of the way! I'll swat the nasty thing!" exclaimed Aunt Gertrude as she burst in from the dining room. Brandishing a fly swatter, she advanced on the scorpion with lethal intent.

"No. Don't kill it!" Frank protested. "It's an interesting specimen."

"Interesting, my hat!" sniffed Aunt Gertrude. "That creature may be deadly!"

"I'm not so sure. Where did it come from?"

"Out of here," Mrs. Hardy replied in a shaky voice, holding up the plastic container.

Frank and Joe examined the label, which bore the name *Vinegareen*. But no manufacturer's name or address was shown.

Joe glanced at his mother, puzzled. "Where'd you get this, Mom? At the supermarket?"

"Certainly not!" Aunt Gertrude cut in, in a scandalized voice. "I got it this morning from a door-to-door peddler."

"Some phony!" said Joe angrily. "What did he tell you?"

"That he was handing out free samples of a new food product. Said it was highly condensed, and mixed with water, it would give a particularly rich, flavorful form of vinegar."

The spinster paused to examine the plastic container. "Hmph. Empty, is it?"

"It is now," Frank said drily.

"I might have known there was something wrong with such an offer. I thought at the time the fellow looked suspicious. 'That man's got a criminal type of face,' I said to myself. 'He'll come to no good end!' "

Miss Hardy seemed as annoyed about being cheated out of the expected free sample as she was about the sinister trick that had been played.

The boys smothered grins, then Frank turned anxiously back to their mother. "It didn't sting you, did it?"

"No, but it frightened me out of my wits."

"I don't blame you. That thing really looks scary."

With a shudder, Mrs. Hardy went on, "When I opened the container, it crawled out on my hand! I had to shake it off in the sink."

"It's a wonder it didn't sting you," Joe said.

"From what I read in the encyclopedia," Frank said, "I've a hunch this is a whip scorpion called a vinegaroon, a kind that's found in the southwestern United States and Mexico. It's called that because it emits a vinegary odor when aroused, just as this one's doing. Many people think they're highly venomous, but the scientists who study scorpions say they are not."

Aunt Gertrude described the peddler as a knobby-nosed man with sideburns, wearing a yellow knit sport shirt and checked summer slacks.

"Neat description," Frank said approvingly. "You make a good witness, Aunty." He added with a slight frown, "Funny thing is, the guy sounds familiar, somehow."

Unfortunately, with no photographs of the Scorpio gang to go on, there was no way to identify the man as a member.

The boys managed to corral the scorpion back into the plastic container and delivered it to the home of Thomas "Cap" Bailey, their science teacher and track coach at Bayport High, with whom they had once searched for fossils out West in a place called Wildcat Swamp. Cap verified Frank's guess that the creature was a vinegaroon.

"It'll make a great specimen for our science collection," he added. "Thanks, boys."

"Too bad we didn't see those guys who ambushed us in the park yesterday," Joe remarked as they drove home.

"Or those creeps on Rocky Isle last night," Frank said. "Then we might know for sure whether Aunt Gertrude's phony peddler was one of the gang."

"I'll bet anything he was," Joe declared.

"Likewise. But definite evidence would be better. Which reminds me, Joe, speaking of the park, we still haven't checked out those two guys Pop Carter mentioned."

"You mean the ones who've been trying to buy him out?"

"Yes."

"Let's call them as soon as we get home," Joe suggested.

After phoning, the boys made an appointment for an interview the following morning with Clyde Bohm at his real-estate office. The animal park magnate, Arthur Bixby, agreed to see them Thursday.

After dinner that evening, the Hardys decided to find out whether or not there was anything in Joe's notion that the mustached terrorist, Jemal Raman, might actually be the fired elephant trainer, Kassim Bey, who was believed to be dead.

"I know it sounds far out," Joe admitted, "but there must be some connection between these two cases we're working on—the Scorpio gang causing the dirigible explosions and Pop's trouble at Wild World. Take that pair who ambushed us in the woods. They warned us to keep out of the *Safari Queen* mystery, but the ambush happened at the park."

"Check. And that's also where the hollow-tree code message was planted, along with the first scorpion," Frank added. "And don't forget the gang member who was hiding out on Rocky Isle. He was reading up on elephants!"

"Right. Plus the fact that those green-light signals being flashed toward Rocky Isle came from the Ferris wheel at Wild World."

"I agree, Joe, there must be some connection; otherwise we're up against too many coincidences. It won't hurt to check out your hunch with Pop Carter."

As they drove down Elm Street, away from their house, Frank, who was at the wheel, suddenly muttered, "Oh-oh!"

"What's the matter?" Joe asked.

"That parked car we just passed back there on the left. The guy in it had a mustache like Raman's!"

"Jumping catfish! You mean he's got our house staked out?"

"Could be. He's not just sitting there for his health. But I didn't want to slow down for a closer look. It might put him on guard, and then he'd take off before the police got here."

"Circle around the next block," Joe proposed, "and come back on the same side he's parked on."

"I intend to," Frank said. "You give him a good once-over as we go by."

Much to the boys' frustration, the car was gone by the time they returned.

"He must have realized you spotted him," Joe grumbled.

When the Hardys arrived at Wild World, they were surprised to see Tony Prito and Phil Cohen on duty near the gate in the green-jacketed uniform of park attendants.

"What are you fellows doing here?" Frank asked.

"Three guesses." Phil grinned.

"We all got calls this morning," Tony said.

"What do you mean, 'we all?'" Joe inquired.

"Chet, Biff, Phil, and I, all four of us."

"Chet and Biff are here, too?" Joe asked, gazing around.

Phil shook his head. "Not now. They work in the afternoon, while Tony and I have the evening shift. We each put in four hours a day."

"Nice going. Congratulations!" Frank said.

"What about you?" Tony asked. "What brings you here? Just out for fun?"

"Nope."

"I didn't think so. What cooks?"

Frank took out the photographs of Jemal Raman and explained Joe's idea. "Even if Joe's wrong, the guy might turn up in Bayport. In fact, he may be here already, so watch out for him. Dad spotted him in St. Louis and thinks there's an outside chance he may be working with the Scorpio gang."

"We'll keep our eyes peeled," Phil promised.

Pop Carter was glad to see the Hardy boys, but after glancing at Raman's picture, he shook his head. "No. This fellow looks nothing at all like Kassim Bey."

The elderly park owner sighed and fingered his thinning white hair. "Anyhow, I'm sure Kassim's dead."

Nevertheless, he thanked Frank and Joe for their efforts and was glad to hear that they would be checking on Clyde Bohm and Arthur Bixby.

Next morning the boys went to keep their appointment at Bohm's real-estate office. Joe backed the car out of the garage and started down the drive. But as he was turning into the street, Frank suddenly exclaimed, "Hey, hold it!"

"What's the matter?"

"Look at those white marks on the front door!"

Joe frowned. "Somebody scribbled something in chalk." He stopped at the curb, and both boys hurried up the porch steps to inspect the strange marks.

"These aren't just scribbles," Frank declared. "It looks to me like some kind of Oriental script. This must mean something!"

"True." Joe nodded. "And something tells me the meaning's not pleasant!"

CHAPTER XII

Green Shadow

FRANK had the same foreboding as his brother about the strange inscription chalked on the door. "Who do you suppose wrote it?" he wondered aloud.

"That's easy," Joe said. "It's got to be that mustached guy you spotted in the parked car last night."

"I think so, too, which makes me more certain he must've been Raman. He could have sneaked back here after we left for Wild World."

"Right. It was dark when we got home, and we went in the back door after you pulled into the garage, so we wouldn't have noticed."

"Maybe we can find some professor at Ardvor College who can translate it for us," the older Hardy boy suggested.

"Smart thinking, Frank. Here—I've got some paper. Let's copy it down."

It was nine fifteen when they arrived at the

downtown offices of the real-estate firm of which Clyde Bohm was the local manager. He eyed them suspiciously as they were shown into his office, and, without rising, gestured curtly for the boys to sit down.

"What is it you want to see me about?"

Frank decided blunt frankness was the best policy. "About the Wild World animal park," he said in a clear, firm voice.

His words seemed to take Bohm by surprise. The manager snuffled nervously and retorted, "What about it?"

"We'd like to know why you've tried so hard to buy Mr. Carter out."

"What business is that of yours?" Bohm demanded, blinking and squinting rapidly through his steel-rimmed glasses.

"Mr. Carter's been having certain troubles at Wild World," Frank replied. "We're investigating them for him, and we're trying to get an overall picture of the situation. You seem to be part of the picture."

Bohm fiddled with his glasses and squinted at the boys more suspiciously than ever. "Exactly what is that remark supposed to mean?"

"You've tried desperately to buy Wild World. Do you mind telling us why?"

"Certainly not. I've made no secret of that. My company believes that land could be more profitably developed into an industrial site, or perhaps a shopping plaza."

Bohm suddenly rose to his feet and sniffed again. "You'll have to excuse me a moment," he said and went abruptly out the door.

The Hardys looked at each other. Joe rolled his eyes, and, pointing to his head, twirled his forefinger rapidly. Frank grinned.

Presently Clyde Bohm returned, still squinting and snuffling. He made no move to sit down, as if to make it clear to the boys that the interview was over. "Now then, I'm a busy man," he said. "If you've nothing more important to talk about, I'm afraid I have other things to do."

"Just one more question, Mr. Bohm," Frank persisted. He was determined to apply more pressure in the hope of extracting a possible clue from Bohm's reaction. "Can you suggest any reason why someone might harass Pop Carter and try to drive him out of business?"

"I've no idea," snapped the real-estate man. "But you'd better not make any such charges against *this* company, if that's what you're implying, or you may find yourself facing legal action!"

Frank rose from his chair calmly. "Mr. Carter may also have to consider taking legal action, if the harassment continues," he said, leaving Bohm gaping open-mouthed at the Hardy boys as they walked out of his office.

Outside, Joe chuckled. "You really took the wind out of his sails with that last crack, Frank!"

"I hope so. He strikes me as a first-class creep!"

"What do we do next?"

"See what we can find out about Bohm and his real-estate company."

The boys got into their car and Frank drove several blocks through the business section to the Bayport Bank and Trust Company, where Fenton Hardy kept his professional accounts. In the lobby, he asked to speak to Henry Dollinger, the vice-president, who knew all the Hardys.

"Howdy, boys." Mr. Dollinger, a shrewd-eyed man with a gold watch chain across a slight paunch, greeted the brothers with a friendly smile and handshakes in his office a few moments later. "Can I help you?"

"Hope so, sir," Frank said. "We're working on a case that involves a tract of land outside of town. We've just been talking to a real-estate man named Clyde Bohm. Is that name familiar to you?"

Mr. Dollinger nodded. "Bohm, eh? Yes, I know him."

"Can you tell us anything about him? Is he an honest, reputable businessman?"

The banker pursed his lips and frowned thoughtfully. "Well, let's say I've never heard anything against him. But suppose I check with our credit department."

Lifting the phone, he dialed a number and carried on a low-voiced conversation for several minutes. Finally he hung up and turned to the Hardy boys again. "The real-estate company

Bohm works for is a fairly large firm. He simply manages their local office, which was opened recently. From all reports, it's a profitable, well-run business with no black marks on its record."

"What about Mr. Bohm himself?" Joe inquired.

"That's a little harder to say," the banker replied. "He came to Bayport a month or two ago to take charge of the company's new office here, so we have nothing on him before that. However, he does have a private account at our bank. So far none of his checks have bounced, and he hasn't run up any bad debts that we know of."

The last words were spoken with a slight waving gesture and an offhand smile.

Frank grinned back. "Thanks a lot, sir. We appreciate what you've told us."

As they drove off, Joe remarked, "Bohm may be a creep, but apparently he operates inside the law."

"So far, anyhow," Frank agreed, "or at least so far as the bank knows. But that doesn't clear him completely. It doesn't prove he didn't have some kind of sneaky part in causing Pop Carter's troubles, like the stink bomb or the phony rumors about the park animals being rabid."

"You mean, trying to ruin attendance at Wild World so Pop would have to sell out?"

"Right."

Joe nodded thoughtfully and scratched his

head. "I guess it's a mistake to judge a person's character from the way he acts the first time you see him, but Bohm sure *looks* the part. I wouldn't put it past him. What's next on the schedule?"

"How about running out to Ardvor College?"

"Suits me." Joe noticed his brother watching the rearview mirror. "Anything wrong?" he asked.

"Don't look now," Frank said, "but I think we've got a tail."

"Since when?"

"A green sedan with a radio antenna on its right front fender was behind us all the way from the real-estate company to the bank. Now it's following us again."

"I'd say that's no coincidence."

"So would I."

Frank pulled to the curb sharply and braked to a stop. As the green sedan went by, the boys caught a fleeting glimpse of a driver with a crew cut.

Frank hastily started up, turned into an alley, emerged onto a residential block, then zigzagged through several side streets. When he finally headed for Ardvor College via a different route, there was no further sign of their shadow.

"Looks as if you've shaken him," Joe said, with a glance out the back window.

"For the time being, anyhow."

Ardvor College was located in a nearby town. The Hardys drove to the administration building in the midst of a pleasant, tree-shaded campus. A secretary told the boys the dean was busy, but would see them in a few minutes.

While they were waiting, Frank slipped out to the corridor on a sudden impulse and called Sam Radley from a phone booth.

"What can I do for you?" the operative responded good-naturedly when he heard who was calling.

"Does the name Clyde Bohm ring any bells?" Frank asked.

"Not offhand," Sam replied. "Who is he?"

"A real-estate man who keeps pressuring the owner of Wild World to sell out. A middle-sized guy with glasses. Very ordinary-looking, except that he has this nervous tic—he keeps snuffling and squinting at you when you talk to him."

"Wait a minute," Radley said in a slow, thoughtful voice. "That tic does ring a bell."

"Somebody in a case you and Dad have worked on?"

"No. I doubt if you'd find him in Fenton's crime files. But I recall some crook with a snuffling, squinting tic who was wanted a few years back on an out-of-state fugitive warrant. Let me check with the FBI and get back to you later."

"Thanks, Sam. I'd appreciate it."

When Frank returned to the office, the boys were told that the dean would see them. He was a tall, distinguished-looking man with a thick mop of silvering hair and a brisk, friendly manner. The Hardys had consulted him more than once before.

"Another mystery?" he asked with a twinkle in his eyes as they shook hands.

"You've guessed it, sir," said Frank. "It has something to do with those dirigible explosions Monday morning. One of the crew is named Maris, Hector Maris, and according to the personnel records, he went to Ardvor College. We wondered if you could tell us anything about him."

"Maris, hmm." The dean frowned briefly. "Oh, yes, Hector Maris. I recall him now. Very nice young chap. Graduated a year ago. He's not under suspicion of anything, I hope?"

"Not exactly," Joe said. "In fact we're wondering if there may be a mixup in identities."

"I see. Well, the Hector Maris who attended Ardvor got very good marks as I recall. He was a pre-med student. Also on the swim team."

"A pre-med student?" Frank echoed and exchanged a puzzled glance with Joe. "Why would a pre-med student apply for a job on a dirigible crew?"

"Good question," said the dean, pinching his upper lip thoughtfully. "Maybe he couldn't raise the money to continue his education. Or perhaps he wasn't accepted at any medical school. There's intense competition among applicants, you know. But let me just check our files."

The dean pressed a switch on his intercom and spoke to his secretary. A few moments later, she brought in a folder bearing the name Hector Maris.

"Now then, let's see what we have on him," said the dean, opening the folder. "Ah, perhaps this picture of him would help to clear up any confusion. All students here at Ardvor are required to include a photo with their entrance application."

Frank and Joe were startled as they looked at the form the dean handed them. The young man shown in the attached photo was blond and stocky. But the Hector Maris Joe had photographed aboard the *Safari Queen* was *dark and slender!*

Frank scanned the application data hastily before handing the form back to the dean. "Thanks, sir. You've cleared up one question, at least. This isn't the fellow we're investigating."

"He's the only Hector Maris who attended Ardvor," the dean reported after having his secretary double-check the files.

Frank nodded. "Which means either someone's goofed in the Quinn Air Fleet personnel department, or somebody's trying to pull a fast one."

"There's one other thing you might be able to help us on, sir," Joe put in, handing the dean the piece of paper on which he had copied the inscription chalked on the Hardys' front door. "We think this may be some kind of Oriental script."

The dean studied the odd markings. "Yes, I agree."

"Could someone please translate it for us?"

"Hm. Yes. I think our professor of Oriental studies may be able to help." Picking up the phone, the dean arranged for the boys to meet Professor Meister, who proved to be an elderly, pipe-smoking man with bushy eyebrows. He needed only a brief look at the markings to translate them.

"These are three words in Hindi, a language spoken in India and written in the Devanagari script. *Hoshiar! Bura kismet!*"

"What do those words mean, sir?" Frank asked.

"I suppose you could call it a warning. They stand for *Beware! Bad luck!*" The professor brushed some ashes off his vest and flashed the Hardys a quizzical look. "Where did you run across them?"

"On our front door," Joe replied with a wry smile.

As the boys were driving away from the college, Frank said, "I guess this practically proves that our unknown caller was Jemal Raman. He's a Hindu."

"Could be," said Joe. "But the language might also apply to that elephant trainer, Kassim Bey. That is, assuming Pop Carter's mistaken and Bey is still alive."

"Pop said Kassim Bey was a Pakistani."

"Sure, but Pakistan used to be part of India, and the two countries are right next to each other. It wouldn't be surprising if he could read and write Hindi."

"Guess you're right," Frank conceded, scratching his head. "But if Pop Carter says Kassim's dead, let's leave him that way unless we find out otherwise. Jemal Raman's a big enough headache!"

When they reached their house, the Hardys decided to phone the airship crewman who called himself Hector Maris and give him a chance to explain why the photograph on his college application differed so drastically from his appearance.

"Of course it's still possible there are two Hector Marises," Joe mused.

Frank shook his head. "No chance. I took a good look at the data on his college application. It matched the Quinn Air Fleet personnel data all the way."

After dialing the air-fleet terminal, Frank was told that Maris had not reported for work that day. Nor had he answered the telephone.

"Looks as if we're up against another blank wall," Frank remarked. His hand was still on the receiver when the phone rang. He answered, "Hardy residence."

"Frank?" said a voice at the other end of the

line. "This is Leroy Mitchell, the park attendant at Wild World. I met you and your brother on Monday when you went through lion country."

"Hi, Leroy," Frank said, recalling the black youth instantly. "Good hearing from you. What's new?"

"I understand you Hardys are looking for a man with a mustache."

"How did you know?"

"Your friend Phil Cohen told Chet Morton, and Chet told me when I was talking with him at the hot-dog stand."

"Well, it's true," Frank confirmed. "Have you seen the guy?"

"No, but I have something else that may interest you," Leroy reported. "Did you notice the two dudes in the car just behind you, when the elephant started kicking up all that fuss?"

"Yes, two wise guys in sport shirts, munching popcorn."

"Right, they're the ones. I came to see what was going on just as the guard pulled your car out of line and took you to see Pop Carter. They were laughing and carrying on like it was all a big joke."

"It probably was, to a couple of loudmouths like them," Frank said wryly. "Why? What about them?"

"Well, I saw those two even before that," Leroy said. "They were in one of the cars that pulled up to watch when you stopped to check out that hollow tree. And that's not all."

"What else?"

"Those same fellows drove through the animal park again today, and they sure don't look like nature lovers! I felt they were up to no good. When my partner relieved me at the gate booth," Leroy continued, "I went to tell Chet. Believe it or not, I spotted them again. They were skulking among some bushes, snapping a picture of Chet!"

CHAPTER XIII

The Sea-Faring Stranger

FRANK was alarmed. He at once thought of the snapshot of himself and Joe that they had found tucked between the pages of the elephant book in the cave on Rocky Isle.

If a gang member had photographed the Hardys unaware so the others would recognize them and harass them, maybe they were now planning to annoy the boys' friends.

"Are the two guys still in the park?" Frank asked.

"Yes. Chet's keeping an eye on them." Leroy explained that their chum had been temporarily assigned to clean up candy wrappers, soda bottles, and other litter, which gave him the opportunity to keep the suspects in view at all times.

The black youth added that he himself would be working for the rest of the afternoon in the amusement park area, and that he would look for the Hardys near the salt-water-taffy booth.

"Good! We'll be right over. And thanks for calling, Leroy!"

Frank filled Joe in on the phone conversation, then the brothers hopped into their car and headed for Wild World. On the way, Joe said, "If Leroy's hunch is right, those two guys could be the ones who jumped us in the woods!"

"Just what I'm thinking," Frank agreed. "And later they followed us to see if we got the message in the hollow tree."

But a bitter disappointment was in store for them. When the Hardys reached the park and went to the amusement area, they found Chet waiting, long-faced, with Leroy.

"What's the matter?" Joe asked.

"I lost them," the plump youth reported.

"How come?"

It turned out that Chet's help had been enlisted by a frantic mother trying to find her lost child. By the time the little boy had been located, watching the roller coaster and smearing his face with a huge tuft of pink cotton candy on a stick, the suspects had disappeared.

"Never mind, Chet," Frank said. "At least you lost track of them for a good cause."

"That's what *you* think," Chet retorted glumly. "When I tried to take the kid's arm and lead him back to his mother, the little brat kicked me in the shins."

The Hardys could not help laughing at the sour expression on their pal's moon face. But Leroy shook his head, obviously much disappointed that his first detective effort had misfired.

"It's a tough break," he grumbled. "I'm sure there was something fishy about those guys. They seemed to be a couple of hoods, you know, completely different from the people who normally drive through the animal park. Most of our customers are families with children or high school students with their friends. But these two were toughies. They looked like they couldn't care less about wild animals. Yet they not only showed up on Monday, when you fellows were here, they came back two days later for another visit!"

"Don't worry, you don't have to convince us, Leroy," Frank told him. "I'm sure your hunch is right. The fact that they were snapping Chet's picture practically proves they're part of the gang we're after."

"And I'm sure glad you tipped us off," Joe added. "This opens a whole new angle on the case."

Leroy brightened under their appreciation. So did Chet.

"What did these men look like?" Frank asked. "Getting a full description of them could be a real break."

"Well, one was wearing a denim jacket and jeans," Chet said. "He was dark haired with a big underslung jaw and a dimple in his chin."

Frank nodded. "That jibes with what I remember from those glimpses in the rearview mirror when we were watching the elephants."

"And the other one," Leroy added, "was wearing a turtleneck shirt and black-and-white checked pants. He had long sideburns and a big bumpy nose with a bulge on the end of it."

The same thought clicked in both Hardy boys' minds. Joe snapped his fingers. "The peddler who gave Aunt Gertrude that Vinegareen container!"

"Check," Frank nodded. "No wonder her description of him rang a bell!"

Chet and Leroy were astounded to hear how the vinegaroon scorpion had been slipped into the Hardy household.

Before either could comment, a voice called out, "Hey, Frank! Joe!"

The boys turned around and saw Biff Hooper hurrying toward them in his green park-attendant's uniform.

"What's up, Biff?" Frank asked.

"Pop Carter wants to see you."

"What about?"

Biff shrugged uncertainly. "Search me, but it must be important. He seemed worried. He just said, 'Try to find the Hardy boys, Biff, as quick as you can. They must be somewhere in the park.' "

"How would he know that?" Joe wondered.

"The quickest way to find out is to ask him," Frank said logically.

The Hardys hurried toward Pop Carter's bungalow. They found the white-mustached park owner in his office.

"Biff said you wanted to see us, sir," Frank greeted him.

"That's right, boys. I had a mighty strange telephone call just a few minutes ago."

"From whom, Mr. Carter?" Joe inquired.

"Wouldn't give any name, but it must be someone at Wild World because he knew you were in the park. Said he'd just seen you himself, near the rides."

"What did he want?" Frank asked.

"Wanted me to get a message to you, but not to call out your names over the public-address system. He was very insistent about that."

"And what was the message?"

"He wants you lads to meet him—alone—in that little clearing between the boat pond and the animal fence. Said you're to look for an old man with a cap, that he's got some important news for you."

"Thanks, Mr. Carter!" Joe exclaimed. "Let's go, Frank!"

"Hold it, fellows!" the park owner blurted. His usually cheerful face appeared agitated. "I'm not so sure you should go there, at least not alone."

"Why not, sir?"

"How do we know it's safe? Something mighty funny's going on around here, and there may be a criminal angle to it. I wonder if I did right, unloading my troubles on you. Maybe some enemy of mine's trying to get back at me and give the park a bad name by hurting you boys."

"I doubt it, sir," Frank replied, a little more confidently than he felt. "If your caller were planning something underhanded, surely he wouldn't advertise it in advance, or try to do it right in the center of the park."

Pop Carter paced back and forth, worried. "At least take a guard along with you!"

"That might spoil everything," Joe argued. "You said yourself he wants us to come alone. If he really does have information for us and spots a guard, he may be scared off."

After a hasty discussion, it was agreed that a guard would keep a distant watch on the boat pond. The Hardys would pass there en route to the meeting spot, and if they did not return within fifteen minutes, he would raise an alarm and the park gates would be closed.

Frank and Joe hurried off to keep the rendezvous. The clearing was well screened by trees and other vegetation. There was no one in sight. The boys seated themselves on a lone bench and waited.

Presently the bushes parted and an old man hobbled out. He was stooped and wore the battered white cap of a ship's officer, with the visor pulled low over his forehead. His clothes looked shabby, and, instead of a shirt, he had on a seaman's jersey under his blue jacket. His face, stubbled with a grayish growth of beard, was twisted into a permanent scowl by a long scar down one cheek.

The fellow glared at the boys intently as he came toward them, looking around suspiciously. Frank and Joe felt a twinge of uneasiness.

"So you weren't afraid to meet me, eh?" the stranger cackled. Then his voice became twenty years younger as he added, "I'm glad you came, sons!"

"Dad!" both boys exclaimed in astonishment.

"Excuse the disguise," Fenton Hardy said with a chuckle, "but I didn't want to take a chance on the Scorpio gang finding out I was anywhere near Bayport." He shook hands warmly with Frank and Joe, and added, "From what you've told me, I figured you might turn up at Wild World, and luckily you did. I spotted you as you came into the park."

The boys exchanged detailed reports with their father, bringing him up to date on their activities.

"You really think the Scorpio gang's in the Bayport area?" Frank asked.

"I'm sure of it," Mr. Hardy declared, "especially after what you two have just told me. I'd better go now, sons, but I'll keep in touch. You carry on as you've been doing, but be cautious at all times. And take care of your mother and Aunt Gertrude."

"We will, Dad," Frank and Joe promised.

Frank and Joe felt a twinge of uneasiness.

On their way out of the park, they passed Chet and Leroy again.

"Everything okay?" Leroy inquired, searching their faces.

"Sure is," Frank assured him with a grin.

"Listen," Chet said, "We were talking to Biff, and we decided to have a picnic here tomorrow evening. Biff and Leroy will bring their girl friends, and you two can ask Iola and Callie."

"Great idea," Joe said.

"How about Phil and Tony?" Frank asked.

"They'll just be coming on duty," Leroy said, "but I'm sure they can eat with us."

"I'll talk to them," Chet promised. "Another thing. How about coming out to the farm later on this afternoon, when I get off work? I have something terrific to show you."

"Okay," the Hardys agreed.

Driving home, Frank suddenly muttered, "Oh, oh!"

"What's the matter?" Joe asked.

"That green sedan's on our tail again!"

"Are you sure?"

"Definitely. Same driver, same radio antenna." As he spoke, Frank suddenly slammed on the brakes in the middle of the street.

"What are you doing?" Joe exclaimed.

"Having a showdown with this guy!" Frank leaped out of the car and started toward the green sedan behind them.

But its driver evidently panicked at the sight of the boy's determined face. He backed up, U-turned illegally, and sped off with a roar of exhaust.

"Take the wheel and pull over," Frank instructed his brother hastily as horns began to honk.

"Did you get his license?"

"I sure did. I'm going in that drugstore to call Chief Collig."

Phoning police headquarters, Frank quickly checked out their shadow's license via computer hookup with the State Motor Vehicle Bureau. Then he looked up the owner's name and address in the phone directory and dialed his number. A woman's voice answered. Frank asked to speak to the owner.

"I'm sorry, he's not here," she said. "Who's calling, please?"

Frank deliberately slurred his own name in replying and asked, "Can I reach him in Bohm's office?"

"Certainly," the woman said. "He doesn't get out of work until five."

CHAPTER XIV

The Yelping Lion

JOE saw the triumphant look on his brother's face as Frank returned to the car. "Any luck?" he asked.

"You bet!" Frank grinned. "It was Clyde Bohm who sicked that guy on us." He explained how he had found out.

"Nice going," Joe said. "We might've known it was Bohm. The shadowing started right after we left his office."

"Sure. Not only that, but remember how he excused himself for a few minutes? He probably went to tell the guy to wait in his car and follow us."

"What are we going to do about it?"

"Wait'll we hear from Sam Radley," Frank replied. "Then we'll put pressure on Bohm."

Later that afternoon, the Hardy boys drove to the Morton farm as Chet had requested. Mrs.

Morton told them with a smile that their pal was out in the barn. Chet was not alone. Iola and Biff Hooper were with him, and so was Biff's huge Great Dane, Tivoli. Iola wore a pretty blue-and-white terry-cloth beach jacket, and Chet's barrel-chested figure was encased in a red bathrobe. He was tying what looked like a black string mop, or several of them, to Tivoli's head, while Biff clutched the Great Dane's collar.

The Hardys eyed the scene with mystified grins.

"Mind telling us what you're doing to that poor pooch?" Frank inquired.

"This is no pooch," Chet retorted. "He's Simba the lion, king of the jungle, and this black wig will be his mane."

"I thought *you* were the king of the jungle," said Joe.

"No. I'm Jungle Man. Get down, you idiot!" Chet blurted as the huge dog reared up on its hind legs and began lapping his face. Standing erect, Tivoli was taller than the boy.

"That critter's really gotten enormous," Frank remarked in awe.

"Right. He'll probably make a pretty good lion at that!" Biff chuckled proudly.

"What do you feed him?"

"Better ask what we *don't* feed him. He'll eat anything he can wrap his jaws around, possibly including Chet!"

"Listen! Jungle Man can handle *any* kind of

wild beast!" the plump performer boasted as he finished tying the black mop under Tivoli's chin.

"What have you got in mind, Chet?" Joe asked.

"Stick around and you'll see."

Joe turned to Jungle Man's sister. "Are you part of the act, too?"

Iola giggled, looking a bit embarrassed. "Chet talked me into it. I owe him five dollars, but he promised to cancel the debt if I'd be his assistant."

"Sounds like blackmail to me," Joe cracked.

"Go ahead and make fun, wise guy," Chet said confidently. "I'll bet we get offers from television once our act premiers, and maybe even from Hollywood!"

"You mean they'll offer you money to keep the act out of sight?"

"Very funny!"

"On second thought," Joe corrected himself with a glance at Iola, "at least part of the act will be worth looking at." She blushed.

Chet sniffed and turned to her with a dignified air. "Just ignore the remarks from the peanut gallery. Let's get ready for costume rehearsal!"

He flung off his robe and Iola did likewise. She was wearing a bikini swimsuit, but despite her attractive costume, the boys couldn't help goggling at Chet. His beefy figure was revealed by a suit of fake leopard-skin tights that strapped over one shoulder.

"Sufferin' snakes! Where'd you get that?" Joe exclaimed.

"I made it for him on Mom's sewing machine," Iola confessed, giggling again.

"You'll bring down the house!" Frank told Chet.

"Think they'll like it?" Chet asked eagerly, preening himself proudly before an imaginary audience of thousands.

"That's not quite what I meant."

"I get it. You've no confidence in the act." Chet snorted. "Well, this didn't just happen overnight. I've been working on the show for weeks. I got the idea long before Pop Carter hired us at Wild World, and it's been developing ever since."

"Maybe you should have squashed it when it first hatched," Biff said with a wink to the others.

With another disdainful sniff, the leopard-skinned boy led the way out of the barn and into the wooded grove at the rear. Long ropes were dangling from several trees. Chet grabbed one, and with remarkable agility, swung himself up onto a high branch.

Despite their teasing a few moments earlier, his school chums broke into spontaneous applause.

"Not bad, Jungle Man!" Joe called out.

Chet sketched a pleased professional bow, teetering precariously on the branch as he did so. "Okay, white princess and Simba!" he shouted down. "This is your cue! Go get her, Simba!"

Biff let go of Tivoli's collar, but the huge Great Dane merely stood there, panting and gazing around contentedly.

"What's he supposed to do?" Frank inquired.

"Leap at Iola with fangs bared," Biff explained, trying to keep a straight face. "Then Chet will swing down to her rescue and grapple with the ferocious man-eating lion."

After several encouraging slaps of the flank, Tivoli finally ambled toward Iola, tongue lolling and tail wagging amiably.

"Trying to keep that mop out of his eyes," Frank deduced.

"Go on! Snarl at her, you dumb cluck!" Chet berated the dog from his tree branch. "Act ferocious!"

"Gr-r-r!" Iola growled, trying to get Tivoli to imitate her. Instead, he licked her hand.

"Oh, never mind!" Chet fumed in disgust.

At that moment, Tivoli suddenly reared up on his hind legs and began to slobber kisses on Iola's face.

"Hey, that's great! Hold it!" Chet yelled.

"Well, hurry up!" Iola cried frantically, covering her face with her hands in a vain effort to protect it from Tivoli's moplike tongue.

"Here I come!"

With a jungle bellow, Chet swung down from his perch. As he did, his leopard-skin snagged on a projecting branch, threatening to strip him down to his underwear!

Desperately Chet let go of the rope with one hand and tried to hold his costume in place. But his hefty weight was too much to support. Losing his grip, he slid down the rope and, with a plop, landed heavily astride the Great Dane, who bounded off into the underbrush, yelping loudly!

Jungle Man wound up sprawling among the dead leaves on the ground, with his costume half off.

His audience staggered around and leaned against nearby trees, rocking with laughter.

Chet got up sheepishly, brushing himself and examining his torn clothes. "I guess the act needs a little more work," he conceded, then burst out laughing, unable to control his own mirth.

Joe flung an arm around his plump pal. "What a sense of humor! Chet, you're wonderful!"

The Hardys escorted their pal into his house, then left for home. When they arrived, the telephone rang. The caller was Sam Radley.

"I just heard from the FBI," he reported. "Clyde Bohm's got a record, all right."

"No kidding!" Frank exclaimed. "What for?"

"Fraud and embezzlement. He served two years behind bars in Kansas and got out a couple of months ago. But the Bureau's got nothing on any of the foreign passengers who flew in Monday on the *Safari Queen*."

"What you just told me about Bohm is news enough," Frank said with an eager smile. "And that's not all, by the way."

He informed the operative about the car that

had shadowed them that afternoon and how he had discovered that their shadow was one of Bohm's employees.

"Good work, Frank," Sam Radley congratulated him. "Are you going to confront Bohm with all this?"

"You bet! I think Joe and I will drop around to his place tonight. Want to come along?"

"Wouldn't miss it for the world!" Sam chuckled.

After dinner that evening, he accompanied the Hardy boys to Clyde Bohm's home, which they found by consulting the latest phone directory. It proved to be a rented flat on the north edge of town.

The real-estate man was at first indignant that the Hardys should bother him after hours. "What right have you got to come snooping around here at this time of evening?" he ranted, snuffling and squinting at his three visitors. "I'll report this to the police!"

"You do that," Frank said calmly. "And while you're at it, maybe you'd better tell them how you've been employing *this* fellow lately." He held out a piece of paper bearing the name, address, and license-plate number of their shadow, which he had obtained from the police that afternoon. Bohm turned pale as he read the information.

"Maybe they'll also be interested in your record

as a con artist and embezzler," Sam Radley added.

Gulping and stammering, Bohm stepped back from the door. "M-M-Maybe you'd better come inside."

Wringing his hands after they had entered and sat down, the real-estate man went on, "My reputation could be ruined here in Bayport if all this comes out. Remember, I'm new on this job, gentlemen. Surely you won't find it necessary to make the information public?"

"That depends on how well you cooperate," Frank said.

"I'll tell you anything you want to know," Bohm whined. "Anything at all!" He then revealed that he had been ordered to buy out Pop Carter's interest in Wild World, using available means.

"Did that include harassing him with stink bombs and nasty rumors?"

"No, no! Nothing like that!" Bohm assured them.

"Where did your orders come from?" said Frank.

Bohm claimed they had been passed down by some unnamed official higher up in the holding company that owned his real-estate firm. "We're just a subsidiary!" he stressed.

After the trio left, Sam Radley promised to trace the owners of the holding company. "But it may not be easy," he added. "The financial structure of corporations can get complicated these days. Often holding companies are used to mask the real owners of a business."

The operative was amazed to hear about the Hardy boys' investigation of the dirigible crewman, Hector Maris. "If he turns out to be the son of Quinn's ex-partner, he may be the saboteur behind the *Safari Queen* explosions," Sam conjectured, "trying to avenge his father's breakup with Quinn."

"That's the angle we're working on," Frank said.

After dropping Sam Radley at his house, the Hardys drove to their own home on Elm Street. As they turned up the drive, Aunt Gertrude suddenly appeared in the glare of their headlights. Waving a broom, she appeared to be in a state of high excitement.

"Help me!" she cried. "I've caught the culprit!"

CHAPTER XV

Aunt Gertrude's Prisoner

FRANK slammed on the brakes, and both boys leaped out of the car.

"What culprit, Aunt Gertrude?" Joe demanded.

"Over there!" she replied, jabbing the air with her broom in the direction of the back porch. "He may be the head of that Scorpio gang Fenton's after! Or at least the rascal who chalked those marks on our front door!"

Joe had snatched a flashlight from the car's glove compartment, and aimed it in the direction in which Miss Hardy was pointing.

A man was slumped on the back-porch steps, clutching his head in both hands. He looked up groggily. The Hardy boys gasped as they recognized his mustached face.

"It's Jemal Raman!" Frank exclaimed.

The man shook his head. "No. I'm not."

"Tell us another story," Joe scoffed. "How'd you catch him, Aunt Gertrude?"

Miss Hardy explained that she had been home alone and had noticed a suspicious-looking mustached stranger lurking on the corner when she went out to the drugstore to buy some indigestion pills.

"When I came back, he was no longer in sight," she went on, "but I remembered what you had told me about that terrorist Fenton had mentioned, so I decided not to take any chances."

"Smart thinking, Aunty," Frank approved.

After scouting the front of the house, she had circled around through a neighbor's yard and had glimpsed a dark form huddled outside one of the Hardys' rear basement windows.

"I retreated to the front porch," Aunt Gertrude related, "and armed myself with a broom I had left out this morning. Then I tiptoed around the house and attacked the intruder. I whacked him good and proper!"

"Aunt Gertrude, that's the bravest thing I've heard in a long time," Frank declared, hugging her.

"You said it!" Joe chimed in, planting a kiss on her cheek.

"Hmph! Well, anyhow," she continued, trying to maintain her poise, "I was just about to go in and call the police when you boys drove up."

"We'll attend to him," Frank said.

After herding their prisoner inside and frisking him, the boys made him sit down on a kitchen chair while Joe checked the contents of his wallet. To their surprise, the man's ID showed his name as Gopal Raman.

"I'm Jemal's brother," he confessed. "I've been a student in your country for three years."

Gopal explained that he had happened to see Fenton Hardy at the St. Louis airport and had recognized him from news photos. This gave him the idea of coming to Bayport during the detective's absence and trying to break into his office.

"What for?" Frank asked.

"I wanted to find out exactly what evidence he had gathered against my brother. You see, Jemal wants to apply for re-entry into the United States on a student visa. So I thought if I could find out what your father has against him, it would help him prepare his case."

"And what was the idea of trying to break into our boathouse?" Joe prodded.

"I learned you two had a boat while talking to some fan of yours on the plane flying into Bayport." Gopal Raman said he had hoped to find something useful in the boathouse, perhaps even a spare set of keys to the Hardy home, which would enable him to slip in easily when everyone was out or during the night.

His spying and the chalk mark on the door were intended to unnerve the family. "That way, if I *were* spotted breaking in," Gopal confessed glumly, "I hoped to scare the women into letting me go without a struggle."

"Boy, you sure didn't count on our broom-toting aunt!" Joe chuckled.

The prisoner was so depressed and woebegone, the Hardy boys hardly had the heart to turn him over to the police. They both felt that Gopal Raman had proved himself a rather bumbling, inept villain.

"P-please don't hand me over to the authorities," he quavered. "I shall be totally disgraced and disowned by my father if I am kicked out of this country and sent home without completing my education!"

Joe scratched his head and glanced at Frank. "What should we do with him?"

Frank turned to their aunt. "He's your prisoner, Aunt Gertrude. What do you think? Should we give him another chance?"

Gopal's large dark eyes fastened hopefully on Miss Hardy. He placed his palms together in the praying *namaste* gesture of India. "P-p-please, Madame!"

"Hmph!" Miss Hardy frowned and fussed uncomfortably. Despite her tart, forbidding manner, she was soft-hearted. "Use your own best judgment, Frank," she decided.

"Okay. Joe, take his driver's license, his car registration, his passport, and any other I.D. he's carrying."

Joe nodded. "Right—I've got them."

Frank turned to the prisoner. "Where are you staying here in Bayport?"

"At the Regent Hotel."

"Our father should be home in a day or two. If you'll promise not to leave town, and to remain in your hotel room until he's able to interview you, we'll let you go for now."

"Oh, I shall! I shall!" Gopal Raman promised fervently, sounding as if he were on the verge of tears.

"Okay, then beat it!"

As the Hindu disappeared into the darkness, Frank shut the door behind him and headed for the hall phone.

"What are you going to do?" Joe inquired as his brother consulted the telephone directory.

"Call his hotel and make sure he doesn't pull any fast ones." Frank dialed the Regent Hotel's number and spoke to the manager. After explaining the situation, he asked the man if he would notify the Hardys at once if Gopal tried to check out.

"You can depend on it!" the manager promised.

Next morning the Hardy boys left home early to keep their appointment with Arthur Bixby, the second party who had tried repeatedly to buy Wild World. The animal-park magnate had opened a temporary office in Bayport while he conducted negotiations.

Bixby was a stout, jolly man, built along much the same lines as Chet Morton. Throughout most of the interview, a king-sized cigar tilted upward from one corner of his mouth, filling the office with wreaths of blue smoke.

"So you two are the Hardy boys, eh?" he said, rocking back in his desk chair. "Heard lots about you, but I never expected you to come calling on me!" He chuckled and slapped his thigh to emphasize his surprise. "What can I do for you, lads?"

"Not to beat around the bush," said Frank, "we'd like to know why you're bidding so hard for Wild World."

"Because it's a good investment. Why else?" Bixby boomed.

"If you're so eager to own an animal park around here," Joe probed, "why didn't you open one yourself?"

"I intended to, but old man Carter beat me to it. I may still have to, if he won't sell out. That's why I've opened this office, so I can scout the area and pick out a good location."

"You don't really think this area would support *two* separate animal parks?" Frank challenged.

Bixby chuckled, but his eyes remained cold. "You're a smart young feller, me lad! No, between the two of us, I don't think so. That's why I've been trying to buy Wild World."

Joe said, "Do you believe it's fair to pressure

Pop Carter into selling out after he's worked so
hard to get the park started and invested all his
life savings in it?"

"Business is business, son. Besides, I'm offering
Pop a good price. I'd even be willing to let him
stay on and run the park. After all, I'm a showman. So's he. A good one. We'd get along!"

"Wouldn't be quite the same for Pop, though,
would it," Frank pointed out, "working as a hired
hand for someone else, compared to running his
own show?"

Bixby unclamped long enough to wave his cigar
through the air. "Ah, what's the difference? I
treat all my employees right. They *love* working
for Arthur Bixby. Talk to them if you don't believe me."

"May I ask you a blunt question?" Frank said.
"Shoot!"

"Do you want Wild World badly enough to
resort to dirty tricks to crowd Pop into selling
out?"

"Dirty tricks?" the stout impresario cocked a
perplexed eyebrow at the Hardys.

"Like having someone toss a stink bomb in the
park on a hot, busy day," said Joe, "or spreading
scare stories about the animals' being rabid."

"I've never resorted to such tactics in my life,
and I don't intend to begin now!" Bixby thun-
dered, thumping his fist on the desk. A moment
later, his little blue eyes twinkled and his double-

chinned face burst into a sly smile. "On the other hand, I play to win!"

Frank glanced at Joe, who shrugged and smiled faintly.

"Thank you, sir," Frank said, rising. "No need to take up any more of your time. I guess we've learned all we're likely to."

"Oh, no, you haven't, son! If you're smart, you'll go on learning all your life, just as I try to do. And just to make sure you don't forget old Arthur Bixby, let me present you each with a little memento of this cherished meeting!"

Bouncing up from his chair, he extracted two small plastic animals from a box on his desk and handed them to the boys—a giraffe to Joe, and an elephant to Frank.

"What are these?" Frank asked, slightly mystified.

"Read what's on them, son!"

Both boys examined their presents carefully and discovered the words, *Souvenir of Arthur Bixby, Animal Parks, Inc.* stamped into the plastic base.

Bixby roared with laughter as he ushered them out the door.

"Quite a character!" Joe remarked drily as the Hardys drove off in their car.

"Don't let him fool you," Frank said. "Under that jolly mask, he may be as hard-boiled and ruthless as they come."

At home, Frank made another call to "Hector Maris" at the Quinn Air Terminal. Once again he was told that Maris had not reported for work.

"Where's he gone?" Frank pressed.

"Don't ask me," the crew chief rasped over the phone, "but if I don't hear from him in the next twenty-four hours, he's going to be out of a job!"

Frank shook his head at Joe as he hung up. "Still missing."

"What do you make of it?" Joe asked.

The older Hardy boy shrugged uneasily and plowed his fingers through his dark hair. "I don't know, but if Maris doesn't show up by tomorrow, maybe we should notify the police." After an early lunch, the boys sped to the Bayport airfield for the blimp ride Eustace Jarman had promised them. Both were eager to try out one of his mini-aircraft.

Apparently the baby blimp had touched down shortly before they arrived. Jarman was proudly holding forth about the craft to a crowd of admiring onlookers. To the Hardys' amazement, its gas envelope had shrunk to less than half its normal size as compared to the gondola cabin, which rested on well-sprung landing gear.

"How come it's deflated?" Joe asked.

"Come aboard, boys, and I'll show you," the industrialist replied.

Once they were seated inside the luxurious cabin, Jarman explained that the helium gas had been compressed and pumped into a storage cylinder. This decreased the lift and enabled the blimp to land.

"For takeoff, we do just the opposite, valve the gas back into the cigar-shaped envelope and let it expand again."

Frank and Joe were excited at the spectacular view as the baby blimp rose into the air, then cruised over Bayport and along the coast. Below, on the blue-green waters of the Atlantic, they saw pleasure boats and commercial ships as well as a warship steaming out to sea.

The Hardys were even more thrilled when Jarman let them try their hands at the simple controls. At the magnate's suggestion, Frank steered the craft inland again. When they approached Wild World, he cruised lower, so they could glimpse the spectators and the herds of animals.

"Hey! What's that?" Joe exclaimed suddenly.

"What's what?" his brother inquired.

"That sign!" Joe said, pointing downward. "It's painted on the ground, right outside the fence!"

Frank gasped as he saw the odd, bright-orange marking. "That's the astrological symbol for Scorpio!"

CHAPTER XVI

The Scorpio Symbol

"WHAT? Let me see!" blurted Eustace Jarman, craning.

Frank gestured toward the spot below. The symbol had been splashed so boldly and brightly that it was clearly visible from the air. It looked like a lower-case *m* with the tail of the letter curved sharply to the right and capped with an arrowhead.

"You say that's the symbol of Scorpio?" Jarman demanded, turning back to Frank with a frown.

"Yes, sir. It's one of the signs of the zodiac."

"And you think this may have something to do with the Scorpio gang of terrorists?" The tycoon's glance flicked sharply back and forth between the Hardy boys.

Frank nodded. "There's no doubt about it."

"That's the Wild World animal park down there, Mr. Jarman," Joe added. "We've already had half a dozen other clues connecting the gang with the park. That symbol's got to be more than a coincidence!"

"Then let's descend and take a closer look!" Jarman said with an air of tense excitement. "Perhaps you'd better let me handle the landing, son."

The remark was directed to Frank, who promptly surrendered the controls. Jarman took over and deftly brought the baby blimp to a gentle, well-cushioned landing just outside the park fence.

He and the Hardys leaped out of the cabin, one by one, and hurried to inspect the strange mark. The symbol was made up of lines almost a foot wide, in brilliant orange phosphorescent paint that looked as if it had been slapped on with a white-wash brush over the grass, stones, and bare earth.

"Wow! I'll bet this could be seen from the air even at night!" Joe exclaimed.

"You're right," Frank agreed, rubbing his jaw thoughtfully. "The question is, what does it mean?"

"Any ideas?" said Jarman, watching the boys hopefully.

"Not really." Frank frowned. "Unless that arrowhead on the tail of the symbol is supposed to be pointing at something."

"Hmm, let's see." Jarman turned in the direction indicated by the arrowhead, then emitted an excited whoop. "By George, you're right! Look over there—under that tree!"

The boys hurried after the tycoon as he strode

toward the tree. Screened from aerial view by the overhanging tree branches was another mark on a bare patch of ground. This one, a wiggly, jagged line that was only about the width of a man's finger, was in white paint and was much smaller than the Scorpio symbol.

"This one is surely no zodiac symbol," Eustace Jarman mused as he studied the white line.

"Definitely not," Frank agreed. "But don't ask me what it is."

"Beats me, too," Joe admitted, after copying it on a piece of paper. "It doesn't look like writing, and it's not a picture of anything, either, at least not that *I* can recognize."

His brother was equally baffled. Jarman glanced at his watch—once again the hard-driving, tightly scheduled businessman. "Maybe an idea will occur to you later. Meantime, I'm afraid I have to get back to New York, but I'll drop you at the airport first."

The Hardys were silent and thoughtful on the way back to the Bayport airfield, each racking his brain for a solution to the odd mystery of the painted markings. Nevertheless, both enjoyed the brief flight.

"These baby blimps are really nice!" Joe said effusively. "They're a lot more fun to ride than a regular airplane."

"And safer," Jarman boasted.

"What do you call this model, sir?" Frank inquired. "Got a name for it?"

The industrialist smiled proudly. "I have, indeed, the Jarman *Hopscotch*. It's delightful for short hops, and very tight on fuel costs."

Both boys nodded politely.

"Eventually," Jarman went on, "I plan to develop this into a road car, so that it can be driven as well as flown, and even have an amphibian hull. It'll then be a true all-purpose vehicle."

"And how!" Joe said admiringly.

"With living facilities like a present-day camper, it would be ideal for family vacations."

"Let us know when it hits the market." Frank grinned. "We'll order the first one off the production line!"

After landing, the Hardys thanked their host and watched him take off again. Then they headed for their car in the parking lot.

They had just paid their fee and were turning onto the airport exit road when a buzzer sounded and the light flashed on their dashboard radio. The caller was Miss Hardy.

"What's the good word, Aunt Gertrude?" Frank asked.

"I don't know how good it is," her tart voice crackled over the speaker, "but you and Frank just had a call from someone named Hector Maris."

"The dirigible crewman!" Joe exclaimed with an excited glance at his brother.

"So he told me," Aunt Gertrude said.

"What did he want, Aunty?"

"He wants to drop in this evening at eight thirty for what he calls a *confidential talk* with you two."

"Great!" said Joe. "If he calls back again before we get home, you tell him we're eager to see him!"

Sometime after five o'clock, the Hardys picked up Frank's date for the picnic. She was Callie Shaw, a pretty blond girl with brown eyes. Then they drove to the Morton farm to get Iola.

"Hi, everyone!" Chet's sister smiled as she climbed into the car with a large basket over her arm.

"Did you bring enough to feed Chet?" Joe asked.

"I brought enough to feed *everyone!*" Iola giggled.

"We'll really have a feast, then," Callie said gaily. "I have a hamperful of sandwiches and cookies, and the boys brought some of Aunt Gertrude's fried chicken and a chocolate cake."

"Think we'll be able to stagger home?" said Frank.

"We may have to," Joe wisecracked, "if none of us can squeeze in behind the wheel."

It was not yet six when they pulled into the parking lot at Wild World. They soon found Chet, Biff, and Leroy in the picnic area of the park. The boys, who were now off duty, had shucked their green jackets and cleaned off one of the tables. They were bringing armloads of soda bottles and a plastic tub full of ice cubes to keep their drinks cold.

Biff's date, Karen Hunt, and a pretty brown-skinned girl who proved to be Leroy's girl friend, Elgine Brooks, were laying out place mats. Then they set the table with items from their own picnic baskets.

"Hey, look who's coming!" Joe exclaimed as they sat down and began eating.

Phil Cohen grinned as he walked up to the table in his park attendant's uniform. "Got a handout for a hungry man? Tony'll be along later."

"Help yourself, pardner," said Frank with a wave of his hand. "We've got enough here to feed an army!"

"Just a drumstick will do. And how about one of those pickles?"

"Anything your little heart desires," said Biff, passing the pickle bottle.

Silence fell for the next minute or two. Suddenly they were all startled by a loud whistling beep that seemed to come from Frank.

"Jumpin' Jupiter!" Chet exclaimed. "Don't tell me you're carrying a portable burglar alarm?"

"Not that I know of," Frank replied. He was as puzzled as everyone else. Hastily he groped in his pockets and pulled out the toy elephant Bixby had given him.

The sound was coming from the small plastic animal!

"Where did you get that, Frank?" Callie inquired, intrigued.

"From a guy named Arthur Bixby, who's trying to buy Wild World. Joe and I saw him this morning. But don't ask me what *this* is all about!"

"He gave me a toy giraffe, but I left it in the car," said Joe. "I wonder if it's beeping, too?"

A look of dawning comprehension passed over Elgine's face. "Wait a second!" she murmured. "I've been to one of Bixby's parks near Washington, D. C. Those animals are sold as souvenirs. He calls them *Bixby's Beasts*."

"But why the beep?" put in Leroy.

"There's a sound device inside," Elgine explained. "I guess it responds to a radio signal—you know, like one of those pocket-phone alarms that doctors carry to let them know a patient's trying to get in touch."

"Funny thing to put in a toy animal."

"Not when you hear why. It's an advertising stunt. The people who buy the souvenirs are supposed to keep them handy, where they can hear them, and two or three times a week, the park broadcasts a signal that makes the animals sound off."

"Then what?" Iola asked.

"When you hear it, you're supposed to call right away, and the first ten people who phone in get free tickets to the park, including all rides."

"Hey, that's quite a gimmick!" Joe said.

"But Bixby has no park around here," Frank

pointed out thoughtfully, "so what made *this* elephant sound off?"

The loud whistling beep, which had attracted the attention of other picnickers also, had now ceased. It was followed by several shorter beeps.

The Hardys wondered if the signals had anything to do with the Scorpio gang.

"Maybe we ought to call Bixby and find out!" Joe suggested.

Frank nodded and they hurried to a public telephone. After trying Bixby's office number and getting his answering service, they were finally able to reach him at his apartment hotel.

"Yep, you guessed it, son!" The man chuckled when asked about the beeping. "I got me a portable transmitter and broadcast those signals so you'd see what a live-wire showman I am. Take it from me, I can double the attendance at Wild World. You tell Pop Carter that."

Frank made a polite rejoinder and hung up with a glance at Joe, who had listened in.

"What a gimmick!" Joe chuckled wryly.

Back at the picnic table, they found Chet eagerly explaining a brand-new idea, which sounded as if it might nudge his Jungle Man act into second place. "Animal balloons!" he exclaimed to the Hardys. "If I could get a concession at Wild World from Pop, I could make a fortune!"

"Wait a minute!" Frank said slowly. "I think you've got something there."

"Sure, I could design them myself and get a balloon company to—"

"No, I mean you've given *me* an idea! Joe. I'll bet I know how that dirigible saboteur pulled his falling-elephant trick. You know those big animal-balloon floats that are used in some parades?"

Joe's eyes lit up. "You've got it! He dropped a rolled-up balloon, and it was inflated in the air, by a CO_2 cartridge!"

"Maybe we should ask Sam Radley to check out specialty-balloon manufacturers," Frank said.

"Good idea," Joe said. "I'll bet it will lead us straight to the crooks."

Leroy snapped his fingers. "Hey! Talking of crooks, that reminds me." He reported that he had seen one of the two suspects at the park again that afternoon. Although unable to trail the man immediately, he had observed him drop a crumpled piece of paper, which Leroy later picked up.

The Hardys examined it eagerly, then passed it around. It bore the name Sandy P.

"Who's Sandy P.?" Iola inquired with a puzzled frown. "One of their pals?"

"Maybe and maybe not," said Joe, who seemed quietly excited. "I've got an idea about this, Frank. We'll check it out later."

When they finished eating, the Hardy boys went to lock the picnic baskets in their trunk. As they neared the parking lot, Frank's eyes widened. *A man was crawling under their car!*

CHAPTER XVII

A Saboteur Surfaces

THE stranger held a wrench in one hand! Frank cried out, startled. Evidently the man heard him. He glanced at the approaching boys with fear in his eyes, then sprang to his feet and darted off through the trees bordering the parking lot!

The Hardys chased him, but soon lost him in the gathering dusk.

"That creep!" Joe fumed. "I never even got a good look at his face. Did you?"

Frank shook his head grimly. "But he saw *us,* all right. We were just passing under a lamp when I spotted him."

"Trying to sabotage our car, no doubt."

"Sure, he was probably going to tamper with the steering or the brakes. Maybe we'd better check and make sure he didn't have time to do anything."

Their car doors were still locked, and after carefully examining the undercarriage, the boys were relieved to find no sign of damage.

"Think our would-be saboteur was one of the Scorpio gang?" Joe asked his brother.

"Could be, but the time angle's interesting," Frank mused.

"What do you mean?"

"That elephant beep went off, so we called Bixby. And you remember I mentioned to him that I was calling from the park. How long ago would you say that was?"

Joe shrugged. "Twenty minutes, half an hour, as long as it took us to go back to the picnic table and finish eating."

"Also, just long enough for Bixby to send a man here to Wild World and find our car on the lot."

Joe whistled. "You think that's what happened?"

Frank frowned and shook his head uncertainly. "Not really. Bixby strikes me as a guy who gets fun out of showing off with publicity stunts and outwitting his competitors in business deals. Resorting to force or out-and-out crookedness doesn't fit, somehow. But we have to consider all the angles."

"Well, I think *I've* got an angle on that Sandy P. note," Joe declared.

"You figured out what it means?"

"I have a hunch it stands for Sandy Point, but

that's not all." Joe unlocked the car and got a large-scale map of the Bayport area out of the glove compartment.

"You mean that spot on the coast called Sandy Point?" Frank asked as Joe spread out the map.

"Right—and look here." Joe reached in his pocket and produced the paper on which he had copied the odd white markings they had found near the orange Scorpio symbol outside the park fence.

The wiggly, jagged line exactly matched the coastline around Sandy Point!

Frank was excited. He clapped his brother on the back. "Joe, that's terrific! You solved it!"

"But we still don't know how Sandy Point figures in the gang's plans."

"No, but we're going to find out. Let's take the *Sleuth* and investigate after we call Sam and talk to Maris."

"Suits me," Joe agreed, "but that's quite a run. Maris isn't due at our place til 8:30. Considering the time back and forth, we wouldn't get home before midnight."

"All the better! The darkness will give us good cover while we look around."

Frank and Joe locked the baskets in the trunk and helped the others clean up their picnic table. Then they called Sam Radley from a public telephone, asking him to check out balloon and novelty manufacturers.

Later the boys and their dates enjoyed the rides. The free passes Pop Carter had given them would be good throughout the summer. The group had so much fun that Frank and Joe were sorry to leave the park before closing time.

After dropping off Iola, Chet, and Callie, the Hardys returned home to await their visitor. Shortly before eight thirty the doorbell rang. Joe answered and admitted Hector Maris.

The young dirigible crewman, clad in chinos and a zippered jacket, was clearly nervous. He ran his fingers through his dark hair and sat down awkwardly in the chair Frank offered.

"I suppose you know why I'm here," he began.

"Why not tell us?" Frank replied. "Including why you're going under the name of 'Hector Maris.' "

Their caller gave a guilty start. "I figured you were on to me. Well, you're right. I got my job under a false name. The real Hector Maris is a good friend of mine, who's attending medical school in Europe."

Frank nodded. "And your real name is— Embrow?"

The young man gulped, his eyes opening even wider. "Yes, I'm Terry Embrow—though I can't imagine how you found out. My father, as you probably know, used to be Lloyd Quinn's partner, but they had a fight and broke up."

"So why do you work for Quinn?" Joe asked.

"Believe it or not, I'm an ardent lighter-than-air buff. I got that from my father, I suppose. He used to fly blimps for the Navy and always wished he could have flown in the *Hindenburg*. When Mr. Quinn started hiring a crew for the *Safari Queen*, it seemed like the chance of a lifetime. But I knew perfectly well he'd never take me on if he recognized me as Basil Embrow's son. So Hec Maris agreed to let me use his name while he was out of the country."

Frank said, "Did anyone else know about this arrangement?"

"Nobody," Terry replied. "Not even my Dad. He thinks I'm working for a trucking company. That's what made the call so mysterious."

"What call?"

"Sorry, I'm getting ahead of my story," the young crewman apologized. "Just before we took off for Africa on our last trip, I got an anonymous phone call. Whoever it was, somehow he'd found out my real identity!"

"What did the caller want?"

"He threatened to expose me to Mr. Quinn and tell him who I really am, unless I agreed to—to do those things that happened Monday morning," Terry ended lamely.

"Better spell it all out," Frank advised.

"Well, he—he wanted me to loosen the muffling, so it would sound as if the *Queen* was having engine trouble, and then drop two items from the gondola as we sailed over Bayport."

"What two items?"

"A smoke grenade and a tightly packed balloon in the shape of an elephant. The balloon was designed to inflate automatically in the air after it was released. Obviously it contained a small grenade or destruct charge in it, but he didn't tell me that beforehand."

Joe gave Terry a scornful look. "Is that supposed to be an excuse?"

"No, of course not." Terry Embrow shifted uncomfortably in his chair. "I realized what bad publicity all this might cause for the Quinn airship fleet, and I didn't want that. I'm as eager as Mr. Quinn to see dirigibles come back. On the other hand, I had to weigh those bad effects against losing my job. I was sure he'd fire me once he found out I lied on my application and was really his ex-partner's son."

"So you went along?"

Terry nodded guiltily. "I had to—at least that's what I told myself."

"How did your anonymous caller get the grenade and the balloon to you?"

"They were dropped outside my apartment door the night before we took off. I found them the next morning. But whew! I was sweating icicles all during the flight to Africa and back, for fear I'd be caught. Then when I saw Mr. Quinn showing you around Monday afternoon, I figured the jig was up."

Joe said, "You knew who we were?"

"Sure. I heard him introducing you to the crew chief. And I remember seeing your pictures in the paper a couple of times in connection with mysteries you've solved."

"Where have you been since then?" Frank inquired.

Terry rubbed his hand over his forehead. "I panicked. I was sure you suspected me, but I had no idea how much you knew. Then I began to wonder whether I should give myself up. So I decided to think things over. I knew of an old cabin in the Ramapo Mountains where Hec and I used to go sometimes. That's where I've been staying for the last couple of days—until this morning."

"And now what?" Joe pressed.

Terry Embrow shrugged and swallowed hard. "I decided to talk to you and make a clean breast of everything."

There was an awkward silence. Then Frank said, "If you're hoping we'll intercede for you with Mr. Quinn, you're out of luck. We don't have any special influence with him, at least not as far as crew-hiring goes."

"I'm not asking you to do that. I'm not asking for anything," Terry retorted proudly. "I came here to tell you the truth, and that's what I've done. If you want to turn me over to the police or report me to Quinn, that's up to you."

After drawing Joe aside for a brief consultation,

Frank returned to the young crewman and said, "We're not going to do anything yet, Terry, until we've cleared up this whole mystery. In the meantime you're free to do as you like about telling Quinn."

Terry Embrow heaved a deep sigh and rose to his feet. "Fair enough. And thanks for listening, both of you." He shook hands with the boys and left.

The Hardys immediately drove to their boathouse. Soon they were chugging across Barmet Bay in their sleek motorboat, the *Sleuth*. They talked little, each occupied with his own thoughts about the case.

Finally Joe remarked, "You think Terry was telling the truth?"

Frank gave a thoughtful nod. "Yes, I don't believe he'd be a good enough liar to fake such a story. Besides, why would he?"

"But how did the gang find out his real identity?"

"That wasn't hard. They probably checked out the whole crew, looking for a weak link. Once they started probing the background of 'Hector Maris,' they realized what was up."

"Guess you're right," said Joe. "And they took advantage of it. Well, at least we've solved part of the dirigible mystery."

"But we haven't helped Dad capture the Scorpio gang yet," Frank pointed out wryly.

"Or unraveled the animal-park mystery, either," Joe added.

Moonlight silvered the Atlantic rollers as the boys emerged from the bay and rounded southward down the coast. At Sandy Point, they beached the *Sleuth* quietly and began to reconnoiter the area. Frank pointed to an old weatherbeaten cabin, visible among the pines. Its windows were partly boarded up or patched with cardboard, but a light gleamed from inside.

"That shack could be the gang's hideout," Frank murmured in a low voice.

"And someone's there!" Joe said tensely.

They approached cautiously. A beaten path led up to the cabin through the trees.

"Wait!" Frank hissed suddenly. "We'd be smarter to close in from two directions. That'll give us a better chance to see what's going on inside."

They tossed a coin. It landed heads, which meant that Joe would approach from the front, while Frank would come through the trees on the left. They agreed on flashlight signals, then separated.

Step by step, Joe moved closer, pausing from time to time to listen for sounds from within. He almost held his breath as he covered the last few yards. Suddenly a cry of alarm escaped his throat as he felt the ground giving way beneath him. Next instant he was plunging down into darkness!

The boys beached the Sleuth *quietly.*

CHAPTER XVIII

A Fast Fadeout

FRANK heard his brother's scream, and, glancing around in the moonlight, saw Joe being swallowed up by the earth.

"A covered pitfall!" he realized.

But there was no time to pull Joe out. When the trap was sprung, a buzzer sounded inside the cabin. An instant later a man rushed out, clutching a poker.

"Got ya now, you punk!" he gloated.

Apparently he intended either to finish Joe off or take him prisoner. Frank did not wait to find out which. He had picked up a hunk of wood that he had stumbled over earlier, and now dashed through the brush to his brother's rescue.

The man from the cabin was just raising his poker to strike. Frank hit him over the head from behind, and the man's legs buckled!

But he buffered the impact of his fall with his hands as he went down on all fours. Levering himself upright, the now-disarmed poker-wielder swung around and knocked the driftwood out of Frank's hand. Then he launched himself with a bull-like rush and butted Frank in the stomach!

This time Frank went down. Swinging his legs upright, he stopped his opponent's rush with two well-placed shoe soles in the solar plexus. As the man staggered back, gasping, Frank surged to his feet and belted him in the jaw.

By then Joe had managed to claw his way out of the deep pit. Without bothering to raise himself from his sprawling position, Joe grabbed his enemy's left ankle, yanked his foot off the ground, and upended him!

The man landed flat on his back, cursing. Before he could struggle up again, the Hardy boys were looming over him menacingly. Joe was now clutching the poker and Frank the hunk of driftwood.

"One wrong move, mister," Frank said coldly, "and you'll be spitting out a mouthful of teeth."

"Hey!" Joe exclaimed. "This must be the knobby-nosed man that Aunt Gertrude described."

"Right. And also one of the guys who braced us in the woods. I can tell by his voice," Frank added. Then he looked at their prisoner. "Roll over on your chest and hold your hands together in back of you."

"Try and make me!"

"You want a broken nose?"

The man obeyed. Frank and Joe ripped some tangled vines from the underbrush and bound his wrists.

"You can get up now," Frank ordered. "Then walk ahead of us into the cabin."

The shack contained a potbellied stove, two bunks, a rickety table and chairs, and a shelf of canned goods. The only light came from a burning candle jammed into the mouth of an empty bottle. A few magazines and paperback novels were scattered about.

"You want to talk to us," Frank asked with an edge to his voice, "or the police?"

"Talk about what?" the prisoner sneered. "You got nothing on me. All I did was dig a trap to protect myself against prowlers like you. No law against that!"

Frank realized there was a measure of truth in the man's bluster. Without having seen their ambushers' faces, Joe and he could not prove that this fellow was one of the men who had waylaid them in the woods.

The knobby-nosed crook seemed to sense Frank's frustration and chuckled nastily. "You goofed all the way tonight. While you're here at Sandy Point, wasting time on me, you'll be missin' the real show near Bayport!"

"What kind of show?" Joe challenged.

"Wouldn't you like to know, sonny boy! All I can tell you is that there's gonna be a lot going on tonight!"

Frank turned away in disgust. "Watch him, Joe. I'll look around and see if the gang left any clues."

The prisoner kept teasing and making fun of the boys as Frank searched. Joe boiled and was barely able to control his hot temper. Finally he averted his glance to avoid giving the crook the satisfaction of watching the effect of his mockery.

"Hey, look at this!" Frank exclaimed suddenly.

"What is it?" Joe moved toward his brother.

Frank had picked up a battered paperback bearing the title *Elephant Boy*. The colorful picture on its cover showed an Indian mahout driving his elephant through the jungle, with a snarling leopard poised to spring on him from a tree branch.

"True story or a novel?" Joe inquired, looking over his brother's shoulder.

"True, I guess," Frank said, flipping through the pages. "It probably tells about how elephants behave, just like the book we found in th—"

He broke off suddenly and whirled around to check on their prisoner. "Joe! He's gone!"

The man had sneaked through the open door while the boys were occupied with Frank's find!

Groaning and berating themselves for their carelessness, the Hardys dashed outside in pursuit. The man was nowhere in sight and the young sleuths realized that he could easily lose himself in the surrounding brush, with the darkness for added cover. Carefully they probed among the shadowy trees. Then a disturbing thought hit Joe. "Frank, our boat!"

"You're right!" Frank muttered angrily. "Come on, let's see if that's where he's gone."

The boys hurried toward the beach. Clouds partially veiled the moon, but far ahead, at the water's edge, the Hardys could see the figure of the fugitive. He was crouching in the cockpit of the *Sleuth!*

"Trying to hotwire the ignition!" Frank blurted.

"He must have had a knife in his pocket to cut himself free!" Joe fumed. "We should've frisked him!"

Their voices carried and the man in the *Sleuth* straightened up. Next moment he snatched what looked like a hammer from their tool kit and swung a hard blow at the instrument panel. Then he leaped out of the cockpit, ran a few paces out into the water, and dived from view!

The Hardys' pulses were pounding with anger and exertion as they reached the scene. "He's smashed our radio!" Joe cried, then peered into the darkness. "Can you spot him, Frank?"

"Don't even waste time looking. He could swim underwater along the point and sneak ashore anywhere among the reeds."

"But he'll get away! There's a highway back inland. He may have a car stashed there."

"Probably does. He tried to swipe our boat and leave us stranded. We've got to get back fast!"

"You think those remarks he made meant something?"

"I'm sure of it." Frank worried. "He said 'near Bayport.' That sounds as if the gang may be planning a raid on Wild World!"

"Leaping lizards! And we haven't even got a radio to warn Pop!" Joe realized.

"Exactly, so come on!" Frank urged. "Let's get the *Sleuth* out in the water and shove off!"

Planing up a bow wave, they sped north along the coast to Barmet Bay, then headed inland to the boat harbor. When they finally berthed the *Sleuth* in her boathouse, more than an hour had elapsed since their departure from Sandy Point.

Frank ran to a phone booth on the wharf, inserted a coin, and dialed the animal-park number.

"No answer!" he reported after lengthy ringing.

"Call Chet!" Joe suggested. "Tell him to rouse the gang and meet us at Wild World!"

"Roger!"

Minutes later, their car was speeding toward the animal park. All seemed peaceful as they drove to the entrance. The boys leaped out, gazing through the moonlight at Pop Carter's bungalow, which was dimly visible in the distance beyond the amusement area.

"No sign of troub—" Joe started to say, but his voice broke off as the frame building suddenly exploded into white-hot geysers of flame!

"It's a fire bomb!" Frank cried.

CHAPTER XIX

A Fiery Trick

THE Hardys were frantic with worry for Pop Carter's safety. "He may be in there, unconscious!" Joe exclaimed. "Maybe that's why he didn't answer the phone!"

"I know," Frank said tersely. "Come on, there's no time to find the watchmen. We'll have to go in over the gate."

The words were hardly out of his mouth when a loud *boom* shattered the night. The ground reverberated beneath their feet. As the echoes died away, a cloud of smoke could be seen billowing on their right.

"Part of the fence is down!" Frank cried.

Rather than waste time running along the park boundary to the section of wrecked fence, the boys scaled the gate as Frank had originally proposed. Dropping down on the other side, they raced across the grounds toward Mr. Carter's bungalow.

The crackling sound of the flames grew louder as they neared the building. Its walls were ablaze and tongues of flame licked toward the sky from every window.

"Hold it! Someone's coming!" Joe told his brother.

A running figure emerged from the darkness. It was Pop Carter, his wispy hair flying in all directions. Apparently he had pulled on trousers and suspenders over his pajamas.

"Thank goodness!" said Frank. "Are you okay, sir?"

"Yes, yes! But how did this blaze start?"

"Magnesium firebomb, from the way it looked." Frank hastily related the circumstances that had brought the Hardy boys rushing to the park. "We tried to call and warn you but got no answer," he added.

Pop explained that he had been roused from sleep by a call from one of the park's two night watchmen, who reported glimpsing an intruder inside the grounds. Pop and the other watchman had hurriedly joined the one who called. Then all three had spread out to search the area.

"Soon as I saw the glow from the flames, I came back to see what had happened. This is terrible!"

The heat from the blaze was intense, adding to Frank's suspicion that it was a magnesium fire bomb. "Another bomb exploded right after your bungalow ignited," he told the park owner. "It wrecked part of the fence."

Both bombs, Frank speculated, could easily have been planted during the day or evening by one of the visitors, with timing devices to make them go off during the night hours.

"What about that prowler the watchman sighted?" Joe put in. "Wouldn't he have touched off an alarm when he broke into the park?"

"He should have," Pop Carter replied, shaking his head in puzzlement. "As I told you fellows the other day, the fence is wired. I can't figure out how he sneaked in!"

"Well, never mind now, sir," Frank said, sympathetically putting a hand on the old man's shoulder. "The first thing is to fight this fire. You're outside the Bayport city limits, so you'll have to rely on the local volunteer fire brigade till they put through an official call for assistance. What about your two watchmen?"

"They should be along soon," Pop said anxiously. "Wherever they are, I'm sure they can see the fire by now!"

"Good! And our gang's coming to pitch in. Why don't you go to the nearest phone and call for help, while Joe and I open the front gate for our friends."

Pop agreed gratefully and gave the Hardys a key before hurrying off. Chet's jalopy was already rumbling up to the entrance by the time Frank and Joe got the gate open. Phil and Biff were with Chet. Tony Prito's pickup arrived moments later, with Leroy Mitchell in the cab beside the driver.

Luckily, hydrants had been installed when the park's water system was put in, along with a water tower to maintain adequate pressure. One of the hydrants was located halfway between Pop's bungalow and a nearby cluster of buildings, which included supply sheds, a veterinary clinic, and half-completed winter quarters for the tropical animals.

The boys quickly unreeled a fire hose, and soon were spraying a lively stream of water over the blaze. They also used buckets to dampen the surrounding brush to keep the flames from spreading.

"Hey!" Joe exclaimed as the Hardys refilled their buckets. "Do you hear that?"

Frank paused and caught the distant sound of an elephant trumpeting. "It's Sinbad!"

"Do you suppose he's just excited by the fire?"

"He's pretty far away to get *that* excited!" A look of dismay came over Frank's face. "Joe, I think we've been tricked!"

"How come?"

"That second bomb, the one that wrecked the fence! It would also knock out the alarm circuit!"

Joe gasped as he caught on. "Which means someone else could have broken into the park. Maybe near the elephant compound!"

"Right! And the whole purpose of the fire bomb," Frank went on tensely, "was to divert everyone's attention to this area, while the crooks carried out their real raid unnoticed!"

Joe nodded. "Let's see what's going on over that way!"

Dropping their buckets, the Hardys jumped into Tony's pickup truck and sped off toward the animal area.

They leaped out at the gate, scaled over it, and continued down the road leading past the elephant compound. In the moonlit darkness, they could sense the restless movement of animals disturbed by Sinbad's trumpeting.

As they neared the elephant enclosure, a strange scene met their eyes. At least three men with flashlights groped about the low rocky hillock that bordered the creek running through the compound. Some distance away, a fourth was holding Sinbad and his mates at bay with fiery squirts from a flamethrower!

Frank and Joe were thunderstruck. But neither hesitated. They scrambled over the fence and charged toward the trespassers on the rocky rise. The men saw them and turned to fight. Soon fists were flying.

Though outnumbered, the Hardy boys were well trained in boxing, karate, and other forms of unarmed combat. Nevertheless they quickly realized that they were up against tough, professional thugs. The melee began to go against them.

Then two newcomers joined the fray. One, a

pudgy roundhouse swinger, rushed in like an angry bear. The other threw lightning punches at a big-jawed crook who had tried to edge around the Hardys and attack from behind.

"Chet and Leroy!" Joe cried to his brother. With fresh spirit, the Hardys pressed their own attack.

"Look out!" Leroy shouted suddenly. "That dude with the flamethrower's coming!" He decked his opponent with a right hook, snatched a hefty rock, and hurled it with all his might as the fourth crook started up the hillock toward them.

The rock hit the man in the arm, knocking his flamethrower into the creek below. With a bellow of rage, he charged up the slope at the boys. The free-for-all took on fresh fury.

Once again, the outcome wavered. Frank, who was trading punches with the nearest intruder, glanced toward the elephants as Sinbad filled the night with a fresh trumpet blast.

A dark figure was running toward them past the three angry tuskers.

CHAPTER XX

Stalled Takeoff

FRANK felt a momentary surge of dismay. If the newcomer was one of the gang, he would tilt the odds against them and the fight might be lost!

The man dashed up the slope with long strides, his fists cocked for action. Moonlight gleamed from the visor of his battered white cap. Suddenly Frank realized who the man was.

"Dad!" he cried happily.

Mr. Hardy's arrival brought fresh hope to the hard-pressed youths and glum despair to the gang as the detective's fists began crashing among them. One by one, the criminals were knocked to the ground or gave up. Soon they were lined up with their hands in the air.

Just then Tony, Phil, and Biff appeared.

"You're too late," Chet crowed, waving his fists overhead like a match-winning boxer. "We've rounded up the whole gang!"

"But we could use some light," Joe said. "How about going back and asking Pop to turn on the lamps in the compound?"

"I think there's a switch panel in the gate-house," Tony reported. "I'll go see."

"Good. And look for rope while you're at it, so we can tie these creeps up!" Frank called.

As Tony ran off, Frank turned to his father. "How did *you* get here, Dad?" he asked.

"I had a strong hunch the gang was planning something at Wild World tonight," Fenton Hardy replied, "especially when I spotted a boat pulling in just below the amusement park area."

"Then you must be the man the watchman saw," Frank said. "But how did you get over the outer fence without setting off the alarm?"

Mr. Hardy chuckled. "Good question. It's twelve feet high. But you see, I cleared sixteen as a college pole-vaulter."

Presently the lights flashed on in the elephant compound, giving a better view of the prisoners. Among them was the dark-haired, heavy-jawed crook with the dimple in his chin who had been one of the two park lurkers described by Chet. Another was the knobby-nosed bruiser whom the Hardy boys had encountered at Sandy Point.

"You were right, Joe," Frank said. "He must've had a car stashed near the cabin."

Joe nodded. "Yes. He was just trying to swipe our boat so we'd be stuck out there all night."

"Too bad you didn't both wind up in that pit-fall!" the man growled. "I'd have finished you off then and there."

"Pipe down!" Mr. Hardy warned, shoving him back in line, "or I'll finish *you* off right now!"

The gang had been looking for a satchel hidden in the enclosure. Only a moment before the fight started, they had retrieved it from one of the deep crevices honeycombing the rocky rise along the creek.

The satchel contained explosives and timing devices as well as several letters and other written material. But there was no time to examine them. Tony returned with rope, and Mr. Hardy supervised tying-up the prisoners. Meanwhile, the boys were occupied with another problem.

"How do you suppose these guys got in?" Frank wondered.

"They probably chopped out a section of the rear fence with wire cutters after the second bomb went off and killed the alarm system," Joe reasoned.

"But that's wild, mountainous terrain in back of the park. How did they expect to get away afterwards?"

"Maybe some kind of off-the-road vehicle. Once they got back on the highway, they could escape fast enough," Joe offered.

Frank shook his head doubtfully. "I'm not so sure. They'd be taking an awful chance of being spotted by firemen or police directing traffic. There'll probably be TV crews and all kinds of gawkers on the road before very long."

Tony, in fact, had reported that firemen and a highway patrol car had now reached the scene.

"The best way to avoid being trapped would be an aerial getaway," Joe remarked.

Frank's eyes suddenly lit up. "You're right! And I'll bet that's exactly what they planned!"

He dashed out of the elephant enclosure. Joe followed, exclaiming, "You mean they've got a helicopter waiting outside the park?"

"Not a copter. Something a lot quieter. And talking about getting trapped—remember how *we* got steered into that pitfall setup at Sandy Point?"

"Well, first we sighted the Scorpio symbol, and then that white line painted on the ground nearby—"

"Right. And remember who thoughtfully made sure we'd see it?"

Joe gasped as his brother's meaning sank home. But he did not waste time replying. The two hopped into Tony's pickup, which their friend had driven up, and sped off toward the outer fence enclosing the rear of the animal park.

As expected, a small section had been cut open. Outside this gap in the fence, the glare of their headlights picked out the dark form of a baby blimp!

The boys leaped out of the pickup and ran toward it. The blimp's gas bags began to fill, and the craft started rising slowly off the ground. But the Hardys struggled to hold it down with their added weight! Joe clung desperately to its landing gear while Frank opened the cabin door and yanked the pilot away from the controls.

Squirming aboard, the older Hardy succeeded in switching on the compressor pump. As the airship's envelope swiftly deflated, the blimp settled back to earth with a bump!

The pilot fought frantically, his face a mask of rage. But, between them, the Hardys finally overpowered and frisked him. He was *Eustace Jarman!*

"You confounded pests!" he exploded as the boys gripped his arms.

"Speaking of pests." Joe chuckled, "I'd say a certain scorpion has stung his last victim!"

"You don't have any idea who the scorpion is," Jarman jeered.

"Yes, we do," Frank answered. "And we'll be sure when Sam Radley tracks down the firm that made the elephant balloon for you."

The boys drove Jarman to the elephant enclosure, using his own weapon to keep him cowed. Then all prisoners were taken to the park entrance, where State Police had arrived and were talking to Pop Carter.

The satchel contained crucial evidence. Realizing their position was hopeless, the men broke down and talked freely, despite Jarman's angry protests.

Several weeks earlier, when Fenton Hardy had discovered the terrorists' New York hideout, they had fled the city by car. A breakneck chase ensued. For a long time it appeared that they had lost their pursuers, but the police caught up with them again, and the gang desperately turned into Wild World.

It was a gray day with few visitors, so the terrorists seized the opportunity to dump the satchel with its damaging evidence. One of them spotted the rocky crevices near the creek and jumped out of the car long enough to hide the satchel in one of them. They planned to retrieve it as soon as possible, but when they returned to the park about ten days later, they found the site occupied by the newly set-up elephant compound.

Jarman, the gang's leader, was furious at this turn of events. The written material in the satchel identified the various members and incriminated him as the Scorpion. Though well out of sight in the rocky crevice, the satchel might be discovered by a trainer or park attendant. Jarman realized it must be retrieved at all costs, or he might face disgrace, ruin, and a possible life sentence for his terrorist activities.

"What was a big-shot businessmen like Jarman doing, leading a terrorist outfit?" asked one State Trooper.

"He was sympathetic to a foreign power and

was aware of the dirigibles' military capabilities. The gang was financed by this power, and he used them as a weapon to attack and ruin competitors," Mr. Hardy replied. "One of them was the Quinn Air Fleet."

"He wanted to make sure his fleet would have the only serviceable airships in the country," Frank explained.

The gang had first tried to retrieve the satchel by breaking into the park at night, but had been frustrated by the alarm. Later they had flown in aboard a baby blimp, but again they had drawn a blank when Sinbad's angry trumpeting brought Pop Carter and the watchmen to investigate.

Joe snapped his fingers. "The blimp was that 'dark shape' Pop saw soaring up and away through the trees!"

"And when we came here Monday," Frank added, "Sinbad must have recognized those two crooks in the car behind us. That's why he kicked up a fuss!"

"Reckon you're both right." Pop chuckled.

Desperate to recover the satchel, Jarman had tried every way possible to force Pop Carter to sell out, including ordering the real-estate firm Bohm worked for, a subsidiary of Jarman Ventures, to buy Wild World.

The Hardys posed a fresh obstacle. The phony code message luring Frank and Joe to Rocky Isle and the Scorpio symbol trick to get them to Sandy

Point had both been attempts to use the boys as pawns to force Fenton Hardy off the case.

The detective chuckled. "I'd say they turned out to be considerably more than pawns!" he said ironically.

Jarman's response was an angry glare at the boys. The dropped note picked up by Leroy had been a deliberate part of the tycoon's scheme. And the attempt to sabotage the boys' car, as well as the vinegaroon episode had been other moves to harass the Hardys.

Following their flight from New York, the gang separated and went under cover. Jarman flashed green light signals from the park Ferris wheel instructing the crook hiding out on Rocky Isle to come ashore and transmit the boss's orders to the other gang members.

With the case closed and all terrorists in custody, Fenton Hardy, his sons, and Chet Morton went to talk to Lloyd Quinn the next day.

When they arrived at the air-fleet terminal, they found Terry Embrow seated glumly in Quinn's office.

"We're wondering if you couldn't see your way clear to keep Terry on," Mr. Hardy asked the airship owner.

"What? This sneaky young thug!" Quinn roared angrily, glaring at Terry. Then he grinned and added in his normal tone of voice, "He's one of the best men in my crew! If he can assure me that there will never again be another incident, I'll keep him on!"

Terry could hardly believe his good luck. He promised good behavior and tried, with a dazed expression, to thank his boss.

"Don't thank me—thank the Hardys," Quinn said. "And by the way, fellows, that pipeline company wants to sign a contract right away, chartering the services of our new *Arctic Queen*, now that they know the real story behind those explosions!"

"Then the sky's the limit for the dirigible business!" Chet exclaimed enthusiastically. "Speaking of which—how about a sky-high malt, fellows?"

Order Form
Own the original 56 thrilling
NANCY DREW MYSTERY STORIES®

In *hardcover* at your local bookseller OR
simply mail in this handy order coupon and start your collection today!

Please send me the following Nancy Drew titles I've checked below.
All Books Priced @ $5.99

AVOID DELAYS   Please Print Order Form Clearly

❑	1	Secret of the Old Clock	448-09501-7	❑ 30	Clue of the Velvet Mask	448-09530-0
❑	2	Hidden Staircase	448-09502-5	❑ 31	Ringmaster's Secret	448-09531-9
❑	3	Bungalow Mystery	448-09503-3	❑ 32	Scarlet Slipper Mystery	448-09532-7
❑	4	Mystery at Lilac Inn	448-09504-1	❑ 33	Witch Tree Symbol	448-09533-5
❑	5	Secret of Shadow Ranch	448-09505-X	❑ 34	Hidden Window Mystery	448-09534-3
❑	6	Secret of Red Gate Farm	448-09506-8	❑ 35	Haunted Showboat	448-09535-1
❑	7	Clue in the Diary	448-09507-6	❑ 36	Secret of the Golden Pavilion	448-09536-X
❑	8	Nancy's Mysterious Letter	448-09508-4	❑ 37	Clue in the Old Stagecoach	448-09537-8
❑	9	The Sign of the Twisted Candles	448-09509-2	❑ 38	Mystery of the Fire Dragon	448-09538-6
❑	10	Password to Larkspur Lane	448-09510-6	❑ 39	Clue of the Dancing Puppet	448-09539-4
❑	11	Clue of the Broken Locket	448-09511-4	❑ 40	Moonstone Castle Mystery	448-09540-8
❑	12	The Message in the Hollow Oak	448-09512-2	❑ 41	Clue of the Whistling Bagpipes	448-09541-6
❑	13	Mystery of the Ivory Charm	448-09513-0	❑ 42	Phantom of Pine Hill	448-09542-4
❑	14	The Whispering Statue	448-09514-9	❑ 43	Mystery of the 99 Steps	448-09543-2
❑	15	Haunted Bridge	448-09515-7	❑ 44	Clue in the Crossword Cipher	448-09544-0
❑	16	Clue of the Tapping Heels	448-09516-5	❑ 45	Spider Sapphire Mystery	448-09545-9
❑	17	Mystery of the Brass-Bound Trunk	448-09517-3	❑ 46	The Invisible Intruder	448-09546-7
❑	18	Mystery at Moss-Covered Mansion	448-09518-1	❑ 47	The Mysterious Mannequin	448-09547-5
❑	19	Quest of the Missing Map	448-09519-X	❑ 48	The Crooked Banister	448-09548-3
❑	20	Clue in the Jewel Box	448-09520-3	❑ 49	The Secret of Mirror Bay	448-09549-1
❑	21	The Secret in the Old Attic	448-09521-1	❑ 50	The Double Jinx Mystery	448-09550-5
❑	22	Clue in the Crumbling Wall	448-09522-X	❑ 51	Mystery of the Glowing Eye	448-09551-3
❑	23	Mystery of the Tolling Bell	448-09523-8	❑ 52	The Secret of the Forgotten City	448-09552-1
❑	24	Clue in the Old Album	448-09524-6	❑ 53	The Sky Phantom	448-09553-X
❑	25	Ghost of Blackwood Hall	448-09525-4	❑ 54	The Strange Message	
❑	26	Clue of the Leaning Chimney	448-09526-2		in the Parchment	448-09554-8
❑	27	Secret of the Wooden Lady	448-09527-0	❑ 55	Mystery of Crocodile Island	448-09555-6
❑	28	The Clue of the Black Keys	448-09528-9	❑ 56	The Thirteenth Pearl	448-09556-4
❑	29	Mystery at the Ski Jump	448-09529-7			

VISIT PENGUIN PUTNAM BOOKS FOR YOUNG READERS ONLINE:
http://www.penguinputnam.com/yreaders/index.htm

Payable in US funds only. Postage & handling: US/Can. $2.75 for one book, $1.00 for each add'l book not to exceed $6.75; Int'l $5.00 for one book, $1.00 for each add'l. We accept Visa, MC, AMEX ($10.00 min.), checks ($15.00 fee for returned checks), and money orders. No Cash/COD. Call (800) 788-6262 or (201) 933-9292, fax (201) 896-8569, or mail your orders to:

Penguin Putnam Inc.	Bill my
PO Box 12289 Dept. B	credit card # _____ exp.____
Newark, NJ 07101-5289	___ Visa ___ MC ___ AMEX
	Signature: _____

Bill to: _____	Book Total $_____
Address _____	
City _____ ST ____ ZIP____	Applicable sales tax $_____
Daytime phone #_____	
	Postage & Handling $_____
Ship to:_____	
Address_____	Total amount due $_____
City _____ ST ____ ZIP____	

Please allow 4–6 weeks for US delivery. Can./Int'l orders please allow 6–8 weeks.
This offer is subject to change without notice.   Ad # _____